THE SCRIBES OF JUDAS

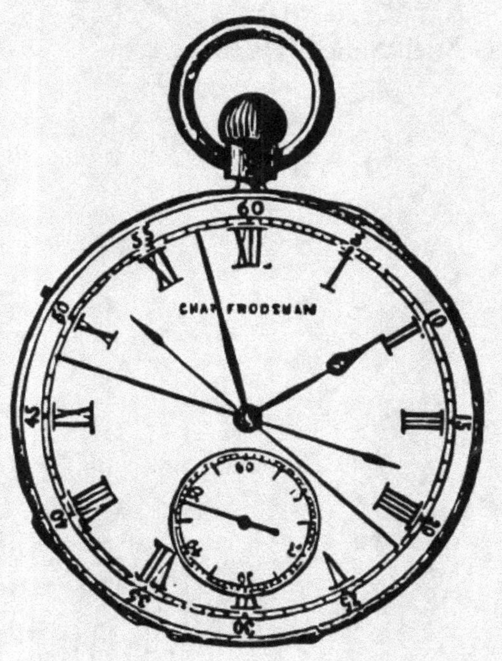

GABRIELLA DA COSTA

THE SCRIBES OF JUUDAS

First edition. December 27, 2024.

ISBN: 979-8230411673

Written by GabriellaSimone Da Costa.

Table of Contents

There are so many people I wish to
lovingly dedicate this.

book to. So, collectively I would like to
whole heartly say:

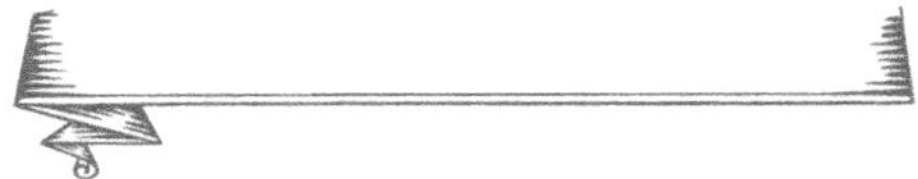

GO. FUCK.YOURSELF

THIS IS A WORK OF FICTION. Similarities to real people, places, or events are entirely coincidental.

The Scribes of Judas First edition. December 31, 2024. Copyright © 2024 Gabriella Simone Da Costa.

ISBN: 979-8230816089

Written by Gabriella Simone Da Costa

Chapter 1
Her.

Where do I begin? Shit. What a ride it's been. Trust me; you're going to want to hear this. Allow me to introduce myself. I'm Francesca Maria Louies Santos—a name that's a mouthful, I know, which is why I just go by Frankie. It suits me way better. Picture this: I'm short, full of bubbles, and, let's be real, I can be a complete jackass—just to keep things interesting.

But let's cut to the chase. Every epic tale starts somewhere, and mine begins like so many others—with a beautiful girl. I was just 15, living in a quiet suburb that clung to the remains of an old mine, where eerie dunes whispered stories from the past and puddles of black water seemed to hide their own secrets. That wasteland became my playground, and I took my dirt bike there with reckless abandon.

It wasn't just about the ride; it was my escape. Perfecting extreme tricks became my obsession, and without a shred of supervision, I dove into the wild without looking back. Getting hurt? Oh, I wore those bruises like badges of honor! If I wasn't bruised, I knew I wasn't pushing the limits. And then there were those moments when I craved a rush so much that I'd dare to take my bike to the road—a choice dripping with danger.

But that's also when I first laid eyes on her. Starstruck doesn't even begin to cover it. Little did I know that this fleeting moment would set off a series of events that would turn my world upside down. Buckle up, because this is going to be one wild fucking ride, full of unexpected twists, gut-wrenching lessons, and the harsh realization that in this chaotic life, good and evil simply. don't exist. Ready to take the plunge with

While I was gleefully breaking the law. I followed the main road back home. That's when he saw her. It seemed like she was walking to the mosque. She was wearing a blue head scarf and then we finally locked eyes. Looking into her eyes I felt like they held secrets that I didn't even know I needed the answers to. It's laughable really, it seems logical that at some point I would end up in Hell. Back then I didn't realize back then that life was much like a game of chess but when I did, I was unstoppable. But if I'm being honest, I didn't give a fuck. I just wanted to enjoy myself. "Salaams" she said shyly. She thought I was a Muslim, not uncommon in our suburb, but I was just mixed and blessed with a year-round tan. Unfortunately, I was in a catholic school, it was a nunnery. I was careless but she was hot. "Hi" replied with a charming smile, she smiled back, and it was game on. Needless to say, I started to take that route frequently. Within weeks we had fallen in love and tried to spend every stolen moment together. I would drive my dirt bike into the street of the mosque, switch off the bike and slowly roll close enough to our tree and wait, making sure to always keep my helmet on and wait for her to finish and then she would jump at the back of my bike and we would till sunset which we mostly spent making out in the middle of the sun-kissed dunes. Out of sight. Laying on picnic blankets. The world disappeared as the magnetic attraction of our lips was too much to bear. My heart had never been so full.

But back to me, Frankie, the mixed short girl that was always getting into fights, always questioning authority, and always doing stupid shit. Because the truth of the matter is I didn't want to be infamous or have power or money, I just wanted to have sex. Had you asked then what I wanted, the answer would have been easy "Boobs." However, we all had our downfall. Mine, if you noticed, was very clearly cockiness. That was my downfall. Well, downfall or destiny, depends on how look at it.

My afternoon followed a very structured schedule. My Master, my grandfather, and my hero had afterschool mapped out for me. A 2km run, then to the playground for the monkey bars 50 on each side. Then home to practice the art of fencing, martial arts stick fighting, and archery, and Saturday was reserved for paintball and shooting. This was usually where I was allowed a break but for a reason unbeknown to me. My grandfather, my grandmaster, and everything I've ever wanted to be insisted, that sit and play chess till I can beat him It seemed important.

Which I knew that was impossible. I didn't know why my schedule was so intense. I missed her but the night was still young. It was weird that I stayed fat though.

I sent a text "11:00" and rolled over in bed, waiting for everyone to fall asleep. I covered my face with the covers so that I could watch my phone. Finally, she replied with a thumbs up. I was cocky about sneaking her in. I made sure the main room door was locked. Then snuck out the extra door that led to the pool roof. Parking my bike there was genius. I tipped around the pool, then jumped onto my and slowly pushed out of ear sights. I started the bike and went to get my girl. She was waiting for me and as soon as I stopped, grabbed her with one arm and kissed her like we were the only two people in the world. She giggled into my neck and got on the Bike, I quietly took off, enjoying her hands holding me. Our property consisted of 4 different houses. Luckily for me, the one I needed was for the most part. Having a key helped as well, we snuck in quickly. My mother has always hated germs. So finally, we had privacy, time, and a real bed. Before I could turn around from locking the door. She jumped on me kissing me like she finally come up for air, we both started to take off each other's clothes and we finally started open-mouth kissing. My body was on fire. We slowly made our way to the bedroom dropping clothes as we went and pressing and accidentally dropping a flowerpot all while giggling. When we finally reached the be, I took control, while kissing I lifted her and excitedly threw her on the bed, her perfect body finally in front of me, and my mouth started watering, finally I got to explore perfection. At that moment I knew that I had my entire world in my hands, and I never wanted to let her go. The softness I felt when my hand ran softly from her clavicle through her beautiful plump breasts, laying next to her I ran my fingers up and down her arm eventually stopping as my thumb pulled her lower lip down sensually. I let my head rest on my arm taking in her body as if it was an exquisite painting that would put the Louvre to shame. I thought to myself, I don't believe in God but there's an angel in my bed. The perfect dream. Kissing her painfully slow between her breasts making my way down her perfect form. Eventually, the teasing won, and we made love, over and over and over and over again.

But as the wheels turn. Good dreams can turn into nightmares. We started hearing the Azan for Fajr. I could hear the phone ring. Her parents were looking for her in a panic. We both jumped off the bed as quickly as possible and tried to throw on our clothes as fast as possible, this was followed by a violently banging the door. Back-to-back, swords up, shields ready. There are many definitions of love but for me, it was rather simple. Love the woman that you would go to war for but marry the woman that wouldn't let you go alone. And what can I say we were in the middle of a shit storm. That was the last time I saw her...for a while.

Chapter 2
God sees all.

This is where I learned that some people are perfectly content to stay in the tiny world they have created in their minds. Right is right and wrong is wrong. But separating us, sending me away for loving someone seemed very grey. The answer was to send us away so as not to disrupt their tiny, perfect, world. I pity them. Imagine living in a world where everything is the same. How small your world is. My parents disgusted by my behavior shipped me off to a Herenigde Nasionale Party church, it was a concentration camp. Isolated in the wilderness. I was led to the cleric's office, and he peered at me over his glasses and said, "If you try to run, we will kill you and say it's an accident." I decided to just listen as I was more worried about her. "Here there will be no fornication. You will attend classes on how to see your husband. You will be assigned a male roommate. You will attend church every day, twice a day. You are expected to cook with the other women. Failure to adhere to these rules will result in further steps being taken as it would show your disease is more complex and will require medical treatment." My face said it all "Take her away" I was thrown into a grime-infested shower, stripped of my clothes, and sprayed down by men with pressure washers, then scrubbed till my skin was red. I could feel their eyes on me and caught glimpses of the smirks. As if my homosexuality could be washed away. An ugly blue dress was thrown at me "Put it on" Once it was on, I was thrown into a completely white room. Part of me was thankful, I finally had a second to think. Flashes of her being ripped away plagued my mind but what scared me the most was what they were going to do to her. I had to get back to her. I had to. In my mind, the only thing standing between me and the woman I loved were these racist pigs. Her pain still flashed, making me clench my teeth as I tried to handle the pain without any real wounds when suddenly the flashes stopped, and my body turned to fire. I felt the fire radiating from my bones to my skin as a hand gripped my heart and squeezed every drop of blood out. I didn't know what was happening. But I knew somehow, we were connected. Somehow. What the hell was this?

I don't know how long I was in there, confused...what was happening to me? Needless to say, when they tried to move me, I was pissed. Kicking, punching "Fuck you!" The orderly threw me over his shoulder and violently threw me into another room. He slammed the door closed and ran to escape, I banged aggressively against the door "You fucker!" My breathing was heavy. "You can't punch your way through that, trust me, I've tried" Only then did I notice a man sitting in a double bed reading, he didn't bother to look up from his book. "So, I guess you're the boyfriend?" I said annoyed but I knew it wasn't his fault. "For us surviving this, yes. You can call James. But that's my dead name." Curious I thought, those words meant the only way to survive this is by playing along. "My real name is Charlotte...and I am a real woman." Her face was adamant. Well, could be worse. "Frankie...I just like boobs" I held out my hand to shake her hand. She took my hand delicately and then I felt it every memory flashing at high speed in front of my eyes but worse the pain. The hurt. I fell to my knees I couldn't breathe. How does this pain even exist? I looked at her with tears in my eyes "I'm sorry" was all that I could choke out. She looked at me like she knew what just happened and her eyes softened. "Do you think that the only out is to die?" She looked at me with sadness "The last boy who walked like a mofie was beaten into a coma. The doctors are not confident. They beat us within an inch of our lives and fight for food as sport...and if that doesn't work frying your brain will do the trick. Those who get to leave, leave a shell of who they were. There's more than one way to die." I paused "How do I feel you?" Charlotte looked at me funny "What do you mean?" I looked her dead in the eye "When you touched me I saw everything, I feel your pain as if it was my own" Charlotte looked confused "I study the different species of human..." She started pulling the pieces of paper frantically looking for as if there was a piece of the puzzle she missed "Maybe a species of empaths...impossible, probably triggered by a traumatic event." I heard her mutter under her breath. Only upon closer inspection, I could see the circles around her eyes and the bruises that covered her body. "What are you?" she said bewildered. "I don't know but this is some bullshit" I was pissed. She looked at me seriously "Calm down" she continued "I want to try something" She took both my hands, lifted them, and put one hand on each cheek.

Once again, searing pain. I felt her pain and this time all those emotions came with flashes of her memories- the good, the bad, and the pain. I was standing in a memory of hers and suddenly I was making eye contact with 4-year-old Charlotte dressed in her mother's clothes getting beaten by her father. I couldn't bear it anymore; I pushed her hands away from me and broke down crying and throwing up. She looked at me shocked "Impossible..." I started screaming "What did you do!" She continued "How old are you?" I picked myself "I just turned 16" looking at her with a look that clearly said, what the actual fuck? "Are you a crossbreed?" Now I was pissed "Yes! I'm MIXED! now what the fuck is going on?" I emphasized the word 'mixed' because 'crossbreed' was just fucking rude. "Your abilities are manifesting; I've heard of feeling other people's feelings but not it manifesting much less becoming part of a memory itself" She looked at me curious. Now I was very annoyed "And how exactly is that supposed to get us out of this situation?" I felt her life and felt that I couldn't escape without her. She wouldn't make it, no one should have to carry that pain. "I'm sorry, I'm being insensitive, this is new, and we are in a warzone." Her eyes softened. "And what the hell is do you mean species and abilities?" She looked at me "You're wanna going to sit down for this." I got onto the bed, and it was surprisingly comfortable but too much had happened for me to even consider sleeping. "Ok," I replied I mean what could be said that could shock me at this point?

Before she started, I already made a mental note to just listen, the fight and defiance in me was calm, like a shift in energy in the room.

"Before we came to our ancestors" I looked at her "Ok," I said. "And they were burdened by many tragedies,' genocide, slavery, colonization, witch hunts, civil war...anything bad you can imagine they endured it. "Yeah, that part I know," I said "Did you also know that all these things happened to eradicate people like you? Your ancestors must have made a pact with some deity that their offspring will be able to fight and not endure the hardships they had to. Thus, abilities started to manifest in your ancestors and passed down through the centuries. Most people's abilities are dominant or completely bred out by people trying to keep their bloodline clean, like Hitler and the Vietnam War. The Americans were so afraid they started dropping atomic bombs. It can be traced as far back as the Crusades. Your people used to be called heretics,' a sin against God, the Vatican made sure this isn't common knowledge. But if you know where to look" I looked at her unsure "So where are they now" I asked. Her face went serious "Watching" Now that gave me chills "Watching they don't torture, enslave or burn you at the stake" I looked at her "All that shit, and they gave me empathy, story of my life" I said defeated. She looked at me "I don't think you realize what you have plus it tends to grow, only they know what you're going to be able to do" We looked at each other and we both fell silent. I wasn't sure if I believed her but somewhere in my doubt, I drifted into a sleep.

I was dragged out of my sleep with a loud alarm. I looked over at Charlotte. "It's shower time." Great I thought. She looked at me unsure "We have to shower together." I could feel her disgust with her body. The pain, loneliness, the suffering at my core it was bearable, my physical strength was coming back, and I felt broken, but those emotions didn't belong to me. "Don't worry, just look in my eyes and we will just do what we need to do." And we did, I was back in that ugly blue dress and Charlotte had to put on formal pants and a shirt. Then we were separated girls in one line and boys in the other. Soon we were set up in a hall each with an iron, an ironing board, and a basket of clothes that clearly belonged to the boys. In the front of the hall stood a tall, butch woman. Honestly, she looked gayer than me. "God created man and woman...Adam, a man, was God's most perfect creation" She walked up and down the aisles as her manly voice echoed through the hall "and created Eve to serve him. Well, that's bullshit but ok. "I am Mrs Koetse. I will teach you to serve your husband in the manner he deserves and cleanse your soul of the depravity that you have engaged in. You will become a lady. You don't matter unless it's to serve your husband. If I see any funny business or a lack of devotion to your husband's cause...May God have Mercy on your soul." Listening to her words all I could think is God isn't here. I felt a hollowness, tainted by regret and destroyed dreams rimmed with an emotion I couldn't pinpoint. Was this my ability? It sucked. I pretended to try but I could see the unimpressed look Kock gave me every time she passed my board. Oh Kock, enjoy it while it lasts.

Once I completed that, in our lines we went off to church hearing the same bullshit, but I can tell you one thing. God wasn't here. Then it was time to pamper our husbands, each girl had been given a list of instructions before being escorted to their rooms. It included things like serving him food and massaging his feet, taking his jacket and a drink in hand for him when he walked in the door. As well as a list of sexual shit I didn't even bother looking at. Fuck whatever demonstration we must do as a test. I chucked the list and threw myself into the bed. Charlotte came in shortly after me and threw herself next to me "I don't know how much longer I can do this." I felt the heaviness of her words. There was a pit in my stomach, like a foreboding but I didn't know what it meant or if it was even mine at this point." You know I am not doing shit on that list" She laughed, it was the first time I heard her laugh." What did you feel today?" she said softly. I went silent "I don't know anymore what emotions mine are...But I did meet the Kock" she laughed from her core. "Kock?" I looked at her seriously "Yeah her giant forehead makes her look like a circumcised penis" We both looked at each other and just burst out laughing. We fell off to sleep and the next day came way too soon.

Once again, I was standing in Infront of an ironing board Kock repeating the same bullshit but this time she stopped at mine "Look at the number of creases there are in this shirt, and you burnt a hole!" she was yelling straight into my face. I had a defiant look on my face but said nothing "How do you intend to please your husband?" now the emotions started bubbling. The pain, the hollowness "I don't intend on having a husband" I deadpanned. She slapped me across the face. My face turned. I looked back at her, picked up the iron, and went straight for her forehead forcing it down till I heard the searing of her flesh and the smell of burning skin. My grandfather had taught me well. That slap would have put anybody on the floor. Before I knew it the orderlies were violently dragging me away. I was brought into the yard, everyone coming out to see the commotion and they proceed to beat the shit out of me. Kicking my face, blood coming from my mouth and nose that continued kicking, my hands bound. I don't know if this was my abilities but all I could feel was hate. I began laughing manically. I suppose that's helpful. I thought while laughing, it was clear I was antagonizing them, but the hate was clear in my eyes. It was clear I didn't give a fuck. I don't know if they got tired or I terrified them, but I ended up strapped to a pole and left outside. Day 1. Day 2. No water, no food just the harsh South African sun, spitting, and the occasional kick. Honestly, it was a blur. But I was so thirsty. By Day 3, I was begging God to take me. I was barely conscious. I knew I was going to die. I could feel death coming. Like life was draining out of me. But slowly my eyes started to close and slowly I drifted away to what thought was death.

I floated down, my feet touching the ground, and when the light cleared. I realized. This wasn't death. This was a memory. My happiest memory. I ran towards the nearest tap in my grandparents' garden and shallowed as much water as I could I'm not even sure I stopped to breathe but when I did. I heard someone in the kitchen follow the most amazing fried chicken I've ever smelt but I knew that smell…it was my grandmother's cooking. I went to the door, my grandmother had passed away 10 years ago, and tears formed in my eyes, as opened the kitchen back door. And I just stood staring at the woman I idolized as she continued cooking. "Sit," she said. She was beautiful, poise, and demure. I always felt her love and protection. I remember that she didn't know the story of "The Three Little Bears" so she made one up. Promising me that no matter where I was, even if she wasn't there anymore, those three little bears would follow me and protect me when she couldn't. I never forgot that story and I don't think I ever will. I sat down at the island, and she turned graciously and sat across from me "Cigarette?" She was so calm and all I wanted to do was run and hugged her "Yes please" I took a cigarette and lit it up. We looked like a black and white photo, two beautiful women elegantly pulling from thin glamour cigarettes. She pushed forward a glass of coke "Drink" she said "You're going to need your strength. She got up and placed the most delicious chicken and rice in front of me lovingly. For the first time "Ouma, Ek weet nie what om te doen nie' I was fully crying. "Hoe maak ek did reg? I was on my knees with my face on her lap. She rubbed my back; I felt her empathy. It's been a while since I've felt protected, my protection, my emotions. No one else. "Jy is my kind. Jy is nou vrou. Daardie twee dinge maak jou die magtigste persoon in daardie kamp." She gave me a serious look "Vroue soos ons kan nie verslaan word nie. So waarvoor wag jy?" I slowly felt myself being pulled away from her she stood there and smiled as I was slowly reinhabiting my body. She was gone. And I was tired to a pole crying uncontrollably. The boys were in a line at the mechanics' workshops. They were silent but Charlotte couldn't stop herself. She ran over to me and tried to untie me. She wasn't even halfway to me…It happened so fast. A copper-coloured bullet right through her throat. She fell to her knees blood coming from her mouth. Collapsing. And there it was. Death.

Chapter 3
The Shadows

Within seconds I saw red, with ease I ripped my hands-free, and with ungodly strength that came with the anger, I sped towards Charlotte and held her "You're ok" I said with desperation "You're ok" I wasn't sure if I was trying to convince myself "You're ok" I repeated. I felt the life leave her body. Feeling death is worse than pain. She looked back at me and smiled and put her hand on my cheek one last time. I was back in a memory, she was standing there beautiful in white, and all the pain and the hurt were gone. She smiled and simply said, "You need to go for it, it's not over yet." She was gone I was back holding her lifeless body, weeping. That ball of emotion within me, the hollowness, tainted by regret and destroyed dreams rimmed with emotion, I screamed out in pain. That emotion I didn't understand, was anger, and match was lit, and I exploded with emotional pulses of energy radiating from me, it was unbearable, Charlotte still in my arms. The orderlies around me struggled to fight the pulse to get to us. Pieces of skin started to fly off their faces and within seconds they turned to ash. I closed my eyes and held Charlotte. After a few seconds I opened my eyes, and everyone was gone. Dust. The orderlies, the victims, the Kock, everyone. Dust. I didn't care. I was still holding onto Charlotte weeping. It was hours that I held onto her lifeless body. Hours that felt like a lifetime. The sun started to descend. That's when I heard the whisper "Get Up...no one is coming." How the fuck am I supposed to pick myself up from this. I imagined the whispers were hers.

Charlotte's body was starting to get cold. It was time. We were both covered in blood. Gently carried her to our room and laid her down. There was so much blood. I was in a trance as I walked to one of the orderlies' rooms and looked for the most beautiful dress I could find. There was an orderly their dust barely held together. I looked at it and flicked it till it was nothing more than a pile of dust. It was at that moment that I realized that the law was black and white but justice. Justice was whatever color I needed it to be. I gently washed the blood and the dust off Charlotte and dressed her in the pretty white dress.

She looked beautiful. I carried her body to the highest hill placed her down gently and started digging. When I was done, I gently placed her in her resting place. I put flowers everywhere in her grave and a bouquet I made and placed it in her hand meeting on her chest. I sat with her for a while, while I made a wooden tombstone. I took a deep breath and started crying as I filled the grave. While I was feeling, I realized that once I was done, I would need to say goodbye and never look back because something in me told me that whatever was happening to me. It was far from finished and I could not look back. I put up her tombstone. I knocked the piece of wood in with a heavy rock I had found. I put more flowers over her grave and the tombstone wrote "Here lies Charlottes. A real woman. I read it one more time and I walked away crying because I couldn't look back. I had no idea where I was walking to but at this point, I didn't give a fuck.

Eventually, a driver let me jump at the back of his truck as he was heading towards Johannesburg as well. It was a six-hour drive, so I finally had time to make sense of what had happened. For long I had fought these demons and shadows that haunt me while I sleep...that whisper...they gave me the strength to escape that pole. I fell asleep and it seemed as if I suddenly entered a meeting. I put my sword down the biggest demon spoke up. "It appears that we have a common enemy" he started "They tortured you...you found your way to the light and you've seen the world for what it is" I kept a straight face "You've fought against but we are a part of you and something is coming, we propose a truce because the Beast that is coming that nobody could even dream into existence. You will need us." He extended his hand, and I shook it. Fuck these monsters. My core at this point was hotter than the Earth. Anger we powerful. 'The whisper...was that you?" I asked "Yes" and replied, "Well then let's kill this fucking monster." The truck I was on came to an abrupt stop. "This is far as I can take you" The truck driver screamed out the window. Finally, somewhere in Harrismith, halfway home. I ducked and snuck to the parking behind the building. It to me

5 seconds to hotwire a motorbike. I drove down the road on my back heel. Passing a man, I assumed owned the bike started choking on his burger.

The wind in my hair and a free road speeding and getting that adrenaline "Hang on bitches, I'm back!" I said with a smug smile, and I'll finally get to see her again. Perhaps an even more volatile warzone. So, I had questions for the shadows 1. How do I control it? and 2. How do I destroy?

It became clear that the fabric of justice was slowly being eaten away, slow enough for no one to notice Law and honor are buzzwords that are simply a lie. I'm not sure. I don't trust a man's word anymore. Life is kind of like a hot pile of shit. If my destiny is written by Allah then surely my demise is as well. So, it didn't concern anyone else. I don't think religious people don't understand people's unconditional love. I believe in the concept of God and hope. I do but I refuse to accept that I am helpless. That it is up to fate/ destiny or god's will. I refuse to believe that If the need arises I cannot pick up my sword and fight. I will not wait for justice but rather hope that there isn't a need for it. Now it's my time to get my girlfriend. I revved and pushed full speed ahead.

After an hour of driving, I pulled over at an old forgotten petrol station. Once I got the car the only attendant there looked terrified. I had gotten that I still had blood all over me. I looked like I had butchered a town. "Good," I thought, this will be easy "Fill her up," I said, and he did so, clearly afraid. I went into the shop and took two bottles of water, biltong, and a chocolate. "This should keep me going" I walked out, and the petrol attendant was gone but the car was full. So pulled off just as fast. I had to get home. I had to get to Her.

As I entered our suburb I didn't think twice about going straight to her house. I pulled up and jumped the gate, it was easy enough as most of the gates in the area were low, and some people didn't even have fences because nothing ever happened in the Suburb of Minefield.

I knocked on the door. No answer. I wouldn't be surprised if they saw me through the window, peeping through the curtain. I knocked again. No answer. I lost my patience; within seconds I snapped banging against the door with my fists "Where is she?" I screamed. I suppose the man, to avoid a scene, inside quickly opened the door "She's not here." I was pissed "Where is she?" I snarled "Somewhere you will never find her" I punched a hole in the wall frustrated. I got onto the motorbike and raced home I drove down the gate. My house was a mansion most would say but honestly, it felt more like a museum. I pushed open the grand doors open the echoes alone brought memories back. I beelined to my father's office. He was sitting in his leather office chair as pushed the doors open. "Your home," he said through his pipe. His eyebrow cocked he asked, "I see your abilities are starting to manifest" he continued without looking up from his newspaper "It cost a fortune to cover up your mistakes." "Maybe, just maybe had you told me about my ABILITIES!!! You wouldn't have to." "Your high school has agreed to let you finish. Thats the only thing you have to do before you take your rightful place at Willowdale Institute as the Santos Family future." They will give you the tools that you will need. And your will be with our kind." "Do you even care that I lost her?" He looked over his newspaper and nonchalantly said "She's human" and "not royalty" he said like it was nothing. "Just do me a favor and keep the body count down, it's only three months and you get to take your birthright in Portugal among the other great houses and learn how to use your abilities properly. "Fuck you," I finally said tiredly. I went to my room and finally took a shower. I tried not to think about it. But if mastering this power meant I could find her. Plus, I would be out of here. I got into bed and started to drift away. The three shadows occurred "Ready to Train? They asked in unison "Yes" I stood ready "What do we do?" The black figure in the middle floated forward "You know how to start" It egged on in a gasping voice. I moved quickly and grabbed the sides of his head, and I was in. He sat there "Well done...now close your eyes and find that orb of energy floating inside you and grab it" This was going to be hard. I closed my eyes and focused turns out it wasn't hard to find given the anger that was brewing from earlier the day. "Good, now a hard one" repeat this memory for me over and over and over again" Never done that one before. "The shadow spoke, replay it in your head, then step out of the memory...." I was gobsmacked, it worked. Once I was out of the memory I shocked the shadow. The other shadows confirmed. "It worked." "Tomorrow meets us at the dunes, we will need space for this."

He said this just as my alarm clock went off. School. What bullshit. The Prestigious School stood proud; money really can get you out of any situation. Exams and even mass murder. Given everything that happened I walked in, and it was like every other school. I planned to keep my head down and get through this without killing anyone. But there's always that one that just couldn't leave well enough all "HI!" she said way too enthusiastic. My head already hurt. "My name is Faith, I'm head of the chapel and chairman of the welcome committee "You're Frankie right!" Good God, she was loud "Yeah," I said, the cringe. "I have class," I said escaping "See you soon!" she yelled behind me. I sat down "Dantes Inferno" now which piqued my interest. The circles of hell. Faith walked up behind me "I know right? The chapel committee has been trying to ban this book forever." Shit, she's in my class. I wondered if there was a pulse that would just push people away. Then I had an idea, I changed my facial expression to surprised "That's weird, my girlfriend read it and said it was brilliant" Her face flushed. I smiled "Guess I should give it go then" She gave me a tight-lipped smile and walked away. And so, fate left as I sat there laughing to myself. They are all so hateful at that mask of self-righteous bullshit and they like glitter for people that are so afraid of the Rainbow.

"Please, Dad! I'm 8, I'm old enough, please, please, please" We were in Portugal for the run hearing something thus a bounty of €500000 to the person who brought it in, or its head. It was a tradition that we never

missed. I was nagging "I told you, Frankie. Only the men are the men are allowed. "Just then my grandfather burst out of the back door, half a bottle of whiskey, finished half before breakfast. He looked at me and said "Do you see that pit? If you empty, it. I will give you €100 and you can come with" Half his words were slurred but I was excited and already had the shovel in my hand and started. I wanted nothing more than to go on a boat! I have never emptied a pit so fast. The next thing knew I was at the front of the ship, and I had a €100s to spend on whatever the day brings. But father seemed hesitant but didn't say anything.

The waves were big, and our luck a storm hit the boat violently. Most of the sailors were excited because meant this creature would be more likely to be seen. My Dad put me in the cargo hold and told me not to come out until he came to fetch me. My grandfather was drunk but the men held the ship steady. I could hear waves pushing the vessel like a feather but suddenly everything went quiet, I thought it was over. So, I opened the hold and walked onto the deck. The sea was quiet, and everyone was gone. When suddenly a beautiful calming song filled the air. I followed it and I found myself looking overboard and there she was glimmer colours of a fish but the face of an angel. She smiled at me, and I found myself feeling giddy. "Where is everyone?" I asked, she smiled and said "Look again" I turned around and sure enough the men were still holding down the deck through the storm, but I couldn't feel it. Like I was on another plain. "Everyone you see here will die" she smiled, I turned around and looked at her. "How can I stop it?" She smiled again "Put out your hand" and I expected her to drag me to the depths of the ocean, but she didn't. She took my hand and bit into my wrist and started to suck, it was like my blood was draining but it was being replaced by venom. She stooped and looked at me curiously "Interesting..." she said and disappeared. I looked at my wrist the bite marks had turned into scars already and I was suddenly back on my plane. The storm had stopped, and the sailors had given up, when my dad saw me, he grabbed me and held me close "I told you to stay *inside!" I didn't say anything and within an hour or, so we were back on land.*

To this day I don't know if it was a dream. But the scares were there, and I never went near the sea again.

Barging into my father's office once again "Right. I'm home and I want answers." "Good afternoon to you Francesca" he replied still not looking up from his coffee. "What are these abilities and species, why do I have them, and why does mine keep evolving?" He looked at me over his glasses, but I was livid "I incinerated over 100 people, I'm pretty much a mass murderer at this point. I think I've earned some answers." My father took off his glasses and sighed "We don't know." This caught me off guard. "There's no way to know when we mix. I fell in love with your mother, and we knew the risks, but it was worth it to us." I fell onto the chair at his desk, I couldn't believe what I was hearing. "Your mother's father has been training you in the discipline of the Temple tigers. We have tried to bring out your abilities naturally and for a long time we thought you didn't have any. Then you met that girl. We thought that camp might trigger it, and we were right." I didn't know what to say "So what now? I'm stuck in High School and if I get pissed off enough, I can commit another mass murder?" He looked at me seriously "Well hopefully you can control yourself until you can claim the Santo's seat at Willowdale as one of the leaders of the Willowdale secret society" I stared at him. "So, I suggest you learn some self-control. 2 months." And just like that the conversation was over.

I was back with shadows when the second one came forward. "Touch my face and see if you can locate when I was born" I touched his face. But with it came so much information I couldn't make sense of all of it, the shadow spoke "There is power in your blood." I must have gotten it right because I woke up in a sweat "One to go" I thought. "Information is power." "Well done. Wait till you see what happens what you can do now." Honestly, I was getting frustrated. I needed to let off some steam, so I went downstairs pulled the cover off my dirt bike, and off I went through the dunes as recklessly as possible. It was getting dark, I stopped and leaned against our tree. I wasn't ready to go to that yet. I could feel the anger building again. "Fuck this," I thought...then it happened again. I sat down, defeated. I punched my hands against the ground clenching my teeth and there it was a pulse pushing the dunes up. I stood up. What if I just punched into the air? So, I did, and out came another surge of energy. "Fuck yeah!" I punched over and over again moving the dunes. Now I had a smug look on my face back I was covered in sand. It seemed to me the more emotion, the more powerful the pulse...and I could siphon that from anyone, which would explain why the pulse was so strong when I held Charlotte. Turns out mixed blood is stronger but fuck it drained me mentally. The third shadow came forward "You've been learning" looked at him "I might have." "It's time I tell you. The reason we are here is because your grandmother sent us." I looked at him. And then clicked "Ouma." "Remember anguish, pain. These will not be your only powers. Tomorrow morning have a conversation with a rabbit" and I was up "A rabbit? What the actual fuck?"

Chapter 4
My reflection

Emotions to me, seemed very unpredictable, I knew I could set off an anger bomb, fight with energy pulses become part of memories and even keep a memory on a loop. Oh yes, and I need a rabbit. What I had heard about Willowdale, was cutthroat, fighting in colosseums, hand to hand and what do I have emotions...oh, and a rabbit.

I got dressed, went downstairs, got into the car, and went to the nearest Pet shop. I walked up to the desk, taking off my Rey band. "Hi" I gave a charming smile "I require a rabbit" The lady behind the desk gave me a flirty smile, I'm sure it had nothing to do with the Ferrari I just rode up in. "Yes, we do she took me over to a table, its edges glass. Some were still pink. "I will give you a minute to decide" I looked at them...maybe if I touched them. One white rabbit lifted his head and looked at me. So, I touched his head, "Help me" he kept looking at me "Why? What's wrong" I thought while rubbing his head and he replied! "When we reach this size, they feed us to the snakes' He thought looking deep into my eyes. "This one," I said louder than I thought, the lady heard me and came to assist. "This is the one, "I said again. "Any name ideas?" She smiled, and I smiled back "Not yet" Thank you for shopping at PetMart. "A brown bag, really" I could hear the rabbit "Prefer a snake's stomach? I thought, "No but it's not like it's going I'm going to run" Ok so I can communicate with animals. "Just relax till we get home and once we get home make yourself scarce because my mother will turn you into stew." My mother was not an animal person. I got home and I let him out into my grand garden, "Knock yourself out" As I let the rabbit out of the bag, I stood up finding myself at the cemetery, The 3 shadows standing in front of me. The graveyard was eerily but I always find comfort there. Peace and restfulness. The middle shadow finally said "Well Done, you have now mastered speaking to animals, you only need one more lesson" I looked at him and said "If this resurrection, I'm out. I don't disrespect graveyards!" The shadow laughed "Pick up a hand of soil" I knelt and felt the soil in my hands, and it was filled with emotion, whispers of the dead "The last rule. You can always ask for help" And just like that I was back in my garden. Jesus Christ.

Animals and ancestors. I passed out on my bed. Emotions link everything, they can siphon, manipulate, and weaponize. That was my ability. So why couldn't I feel her? Maybe she's cloaked or witchcraft.

I was back at school, and word at spread that I was gay. Someone came up to me and asked and I burst out laughing manically. Shit if only you knew that the gay part was the only normal part of me, but I could feel the hate. The school was hosting its annual Swimming Gala. I sat on the grandstands. My legs spread out and my elbows against the upper level. Anybody would tell you I looked like I didn't give a fuck. All the girls were in the pool when the teacher approached me. God making small talk is painful. "Hi there Francesca" he started "Hi" I gave a smile that said, 'Just leave me alone.' He didn't take the hint. "Listen I can see you're deep in thought and I was wondering if maybe you wanted to go sit in one of the classrooms or maybe the restaurant?" He looked at me trying to seem confident "And why would I do that?" I said with a false sense of respect. He looked like he was starting to sweat "The girls are complaining that you're making them feel uncomfortable. So, if you don't move, I will have to suspend you" I looked forward. The girls were standing on the other side of the Olympic Size Pool. I focused my core and let a pulse of hate, every drop of water splashed out of the pool, like a giant wave. The girls started screaming being covered in the giant wave. I looked at the teacher "No problem, Sir. Seems a bit dry here anyway." I got up went straight to the parking lot outside the school and revered my Ferrari as loud as could while leaving. Bitches wasting my time.

Rumors started rolling around that I was a witch. Part of me considered fuelling the rumors because I wanted to see just how stupid they were. But my little stunt drew unwanted attention and before I knew it, I was being called into the Rectors office he cleared his throat "I spoke to your parents" Honestly at that point, I thought my parents cared about who I killed. "Your friends and family are worried about you. They feel you have lost your way." Flashbacks from the camp came flooding back. Losing my train of thought I was pulled back at restrained with rope. Yip flashbacks except they kept throwing water at me. I didn't react because I was losing consciousness, that was a lot of hate to ingest.

I woke up on an altar. My hands and feet are tied to the corners. I was so tired I figured let them do their thing, plus I wanted to see how this played out. I mean...they were pretty stupid; they couldn't honestly think they could pull something like this off. I still had a smug look on my face, and I could see it was making Faith stumble while reading the bible, I started giggling that they bound my mouth and held my nose closed. My heart stopped. I think they realized what they had done and dumped the body in a nearby lake. Sloppy honestly. But that escalated very quickly I thought exorcisms were meant to be fun.

I woke up with a handkerchief they had shoved down my throat. I looked at it and put it in my pocket. It seemed as though they banished me to the 7th circle of hell. The scorching hot sand, under a rain of fire people running through the sand without stopping, it was unmistakeable. Guess Dantes Inferno wasn't a bad idea. Weirdly enough I didn't feel the heat only my core energizing, I grabbed a man running frantically "Person of Lut?" I had him by the neck of his shirt "Yes" I looked at him and asked, "Where's the door to the next level?" He pointed to an elevator and loosened my grip, the trails to "purgatory are impossible" he told me "No one has ever escaped" I got into the elevator and said, "That's ok, I'm not looking to escape..." He looked at me confused "I'm going down." I pressed the number 9, and the doors closed. He looked shocked before the rain of fire started coming down on him again. "Lake Cocytus, the lake of lamentations here we come" I muttered to myself. A big part of me wanted to stay, the love of my life was gone, and I was surrounded by people who were constantly trying to kill me.

I heard a "Ding" Well let's see how this goes. From heresy to treachery in 2 minutes. How easy is it to be a sinner? In the center of our treacherous shit show sat Lucifer, the idiot that thought he could take out God. Now I don't know much about this Mafia shit but even I could have told to that is the worst idea...I cocked, my head history or history's first bad idea?" Heads hanging, bodies in ice as I was walking, I could hear the singe of the heat coming from shoes.

I made my way to the center to where he stood. Looking he looked like an ordinary man with a charming. His hand in his pocket was very suave. Other than that, it was rather underwhelming well compared to the rest the rest of hell not mention, honestly, he just looked like a hedge fund investor...or a Bitcoin millionaire.

I hope I have enough juice for this, I guess either way I'm dead right? I went behind him and readied myself, literally only God and the devil know what I'm about to feel. I think when adults said they needed a drink, this is what they meant. I grabbed onto both sides of his and I was in. He was sitting on a leather couch, in what looked like an empty gentlemen's lounge. I looked at him and didn't even wait for him to start "Where's the whiskey?" I headed straight to the bar, I grabbed a bottle, opened it, and took a swig. Whiskey burnt but the more I drank the better it tasted. He looked at me with disgust. I grabbed an extra bottle and made my way to the couch opposite him, my body language clearly showing defeat, so I made myself comfortable. He finally spoke, "You should fear me." He said holding back the anger and clenching his jaw. I looked at him unbothered "And why is that?" he looked taken back "Because I'm Lucifer, ruler of hell" he spoke dramatically intending to scare me "Oh...well the last time I checked, only one of us was here out of the free will and the other is a block of ice" I said nonchalantly. He grabbed the bottle on the table opened it and took a swig "So what do you want? To make a deal with the Devil?" I chuckled at that "Why would need to make a deal when I hold all the cards? You're trapped. Not me." We kept drinking "So what you just wanted to have a drink with the Devil?" he said realizing his tone of voice wasn't working "Not exactly...I needed a friend and last time I checked so did you" I said thoughtfully, he snarled back "I don't need anyone". "You're a block of ice?" I deadpanned.

He looked at me "Fair enough...how did you end up here" asked another swig "Didn't you hear? It's an absolute shit show, I lost the only friend I've ever had, the woman I love is cloaked or whatever, the Christians are constantly trying to kill me and I'm soaking up emotions like it's going out of fashion and I'm drunk in the 9th circle of hell..." After a few seconds we looked at each other and burst out laughing "Ok we can be friends" he said still laughing "BFF" I laughed harder. The fireplace lit up and as we continued laughing into the night, eventually he took out his cigars. I inhaled and exhaled "Well this is heavenly" both of us laughing crassly. Then a peace came over the room and we both fell still. "What am I going to do?" I smiled and laughed "Wanna make a deal with the Devil?" I laughed but he looked at me seriously.

I sat up, well I don't do deals, but I have a feeling that your venom runs through my veins, and met one of your sirens... but I think a restructure is needed, it's a shitshow up there, plus Cheeto just got re-elected. Everybody is killing each other." I paused "But I'm not an idiot. I've been playing checkers when the rest of the world is playing chess and all it got me was dead at the bottom of a lake." He looked at me with a look that said "Fair." "Here's the deal, link my life to yours" he cocked his head "Mutually assured destruction. I'm impressed." I smirked. "I don't want a deal. I want a partnership." He took out a knife and cut deep into his palm, he then held the knife out "I agree" I took a swig of my whiskey took the knife and I did the same. We shook hands and an unstoppable pulse erupted. I had never felt more powerful. "Two lives linked" he started "My power is your power, and your empathy is my empathy, you die, I die." Something that felt like an earthquake. He smirked "Time to restructure" I laughed let's do it. "I will be back; I have Christians to torture" For the first time I jumped through time. It felt amazing. I was back in my body, and I forcefully flew out of the water.

Covered in mud I walked past the receptionist, who tried to stop me still wet and covered in mud. The rector was having a meeting with my parents and the girls that assisted. I stormed in "You're late" My father said "Traffic" I replied. I pulled out the handkerchief that was stuck in my throat "You must have dropped this and put it in front of the rector on his desk." They honestly looked like they were about to shit themselves. Good because I haven't decided what I was going to do to them yet.

Chapter 5
Hell Hath, no Fury...

WHEN WE WENT HOME, I go my Ferrari and revered off. My mother and father were already there. They looked at me "Anything we need to clean" I laughed as I took off my uniform covered in mud. "No, it's sorted." They were apathetic "I think it's time to take your place at Willowdale. My back to them as I continued undressing, I smiled to myself "I couldn't agree more" I don't think they expected that. I put a towel on walked to the bar and took out a bottle of whiskey, I opened it took a swig grabbed the bottle, and started to walk to my room. My mother finally cracked "What is wrong with you?" she looked at me with tears. I looked at her confused "Kill me once shame on me, kill me twice shame on me.... It's time I leave." I continued walking "You never tired me to the pole; you just sent me there. You didn't suffocate me and dump my body in a lake, you just sent me there..." They looked guilty whether you awarded me my seat at Willowdale or not. Come tomorrow. I'm gone" My father stepped forward "We do love you; you know that right? I was pulling out an old Stones t-shirt to sleep in. The shadows and I had much to discuss. "If you love me then tell me where she is?" My father and mother looked at each other. My mother with tears rolling down her cheek said slowly "She's dead...that's why can't feel her. It has nothing to do with a cloaking spell." Her words were soft and filled with regret and for a few seconds, we just looked at each other. My father cleared his throat "You're right we handled this poorly. Tomorrow all arrangements will be made to claim the Santos legacy at Willowdale." I turned my back like I was looking for something. "Very well, now I can finally leave this circus behind" They stood a bit longer, expectation hanging in the air, but if she was gone, I had nothing more to say to them. Like a sword through my heart "What's the point now?" I thought.

Just then I heard a whisper "Come Down," "Why not I thought, I'm getting blackout drunk tonight" I focused my energy and jumped down to Purgatory and shit was I surprised beautiful woman everywhere, Kendrick playing, the drugs and the boozes following, the beautiful. "There she is!" Lucifer said and handed me a bottle "Shit news, I know but I think I know what will cheer you up. "You turned purgatory into a club?" He laughed "Yes, it was boring as fuck. But I think you will be happy with some of the other changes I've made" He smirked. I laughed "Ok then" Couldn't get any worse right? We dropped down a level and I saw what appeared to be the fight club. Lu Looked at me "The violent, the unjust, and any fucker that ever hurt the innocent, wife beaters and such doomed to fight for eternity" We dropped down a level. This one had the fires of hell and people screaming as they burnt over and over again. I looked at Lu, and he replied with "The sodomites, pedophiles" he turned around "Not the homosexuals" he added "and jackass priests and false prophets that talk shit, thanks to you I don't have to deal with the bullshit of condemning love and other bullshit...like the crop thing." He said seriously and again I couldn't help but laugh "But back to cheering you up" A centaur approached us with bows and swords "Since we are with these predators, I thought a hunt might be fun, do you want to do one at a time or all," He said readying his bow "One at a time sounds good" He released one from the flames, the hunter now became the hunted. Both of us aimed each arrow hitting both of his eyes and back to the fames he went. The end of arrows sticking out of both his eyes. We jumped back into purgatory "Lu, I don't want to talk about it." He followed me "I know but I have something for you" he pulled out a small leather pouch, I looked inside "There's like a whole house in here, with a library" he smirked "I know, I don't get the library part, no one reads anymore" I looked at him laughed "That's literally how I got the map to hell" he laughed "Fair enough, plus now you have the time and power to go hunting for those relics you want for absolutely no reason" I looked at him " I hate that you're in my head." I said unimpressed "Oh one more thing" he whipped out a sword "I know that you know how to use it, but this one sends them straight to hell" He smiled expectantly, I looked at him, gave a small smile, and said "Let's fuck this shit up" and laughed " Yassss Queen" I burst out laughing "Rupaul huh?" we looked at each other and burst out laughing. It felt good having a friend. I put the sword into the pouch and put the pouch on my belt. I that's where it was going to stay, even while I was sleeping. It never left my side.

And so, the party started downing shots, dancing on tables making out with well...everyone. I think at one stage one girl was kissing my neck and the other my mouth. Well go figure, no one throws a party like the devil at a gentlemen's club. "I gotta go, got a plane to catch," I told him slurring. I jumped back up. Thank God when I jumped it was outside of time and space. I fell into my bed and slept like the dead.

I woke up Henry shaking me, Henry was my butler/babysitter. Showered, threw on my leather jacket, my vans, and Rey bands to hide the obvious hangover, and followed Henry to the black car taking me to the jet. As I boarded, I got a text message, "Get your ass down here now! I am knee-deep shit!" I laughed and replied, "Well look who got a phone, give me five." We boarded and I headed straight for a private compartment pretending I was going back to sleep. Once we took off, I jumped down and came down to a gentlemen's club filled with crying babies. Like actual human, crying babies. The centaurs and the demon's trying to placate them. That's a picture I thought I would never see. Lu looked frantic and yelled at me "Where were you? It's all hands on deck!" I relaxed and focused my core energy and within seconds the babies were asleep" Lu looked beyond relieved "Why are there babies everywhere?" I asked him like it was a ridiculous question. "Unbaptized" he gritted his teeth. I looked around and eventually said "Guess you have to install a nursery now" I laughed quietly. "Relax I am kidding. So, you're telling me that these babies only sin was coming out of a vagina?" Again, this sounded ridiculous. Lu frantically poured himself a drink." I'll have to create another layer" I looked at him with gritted teeth "No, you don't. How do I get to the gates of heaven?" He looked at me "There is no way in hell I will go crawling back to father!" he was adamant "Keep your voice down, and this isn't about your father, this is about the fact that this is bullshit. Babies don't belong in hell!" "Who stands at the gate?" I asked " Peter...or Saint Peter, jackass in a very saint-like manner sent babies to hell" I looked at him "Put each of them on a cloud" I yawned " I'll text when I'm ready."

He looked at me gobsmacked "Now how do I go up? " He clenched his jaws " The elevator from purgatory will take you to the line." He said almost like he didn't believe me "Perfect" I smiled. Wait what weapons do we have, God knows we don't want him here" I knew he could feel my calm, but I could feel his apprehension, like is this chick for real? He could also sense that I didn't have a lot of rules but the ones I did have, I would raise hell to uphold.

I got into the elevator "Going up." And with a 'ting,' I was off. They must have an alarm or something. Because when I got there, the line was hidden. I walked up to the man standing at the gate "Underwhelming" I muttered to myself. I put on a fake smile "Hi there, Frankie, nice to meet you." I put out my hand to shake his. He gave me a look that could kill and spat at my feet. "Oooook," I said, "There seems to be a misunderstanding" He didn't say anything. Just sneered. Great Guy. "Unfortunately, due to a policy change in Hell, we are required to place babies aged up until 7 where they are meant to be" He laughed at me. Big mistake. I grabbed him by his collar, my face right by his, my teeth clenching. "Listen here you little fucker, I have been very patient with you, people. Now I'm going cut your dick off and shove it so far down your throat that it will come out your ass." I pulled out a knife pushing him on his back. Pulled his pant off and sliced his peanut dick, and proceed to push down his throat. It was so gratifying. I put my face near him again "Now you're gonna shut the fuck up and let me do what I need otherwise I will cut your tongue out and shove it up your ass. Shouldn't be new to you people, always talking out your ass." He was on the floor screaming in pain. Little bitch. I stepped over him and took a look at the pearly gates. Pearl, I thought. Not the strongest. With one forward kick, the pulse of hate and anger blew the gates open. I took my phone out of my pocket and sent a text "Now" and slowly sleeping babies ascended on soft clouds. Just then a woman appeared. I looked at her ready to fight. She smiled and said something unexpected "Soon" she said kindly, with soft words "The gates will remain open until they are all here, but dont worry" She smiled again "He'll be down soon". This caught me off guard. I didn't want to look in heaven. I was tempted in the hopes of seeing her, but I turned around and never looked back. I jumped back to the plane. And got some sleep.

When I woke, I had endless text messages "You absolute fucking legend!!!!" and "Call me back bitch, you just made history!" and "Call me back, we woke up Micheal." Who the fuck is Michael. I put my phone back in my pocket.

I was finally standing in front of The Willowdale Institute. Micheal would have to wait. I was welcomed by the principal, and he walked me through the old building. It's exactly what you would have expected, old money, Mahoney, and leather. Crests, portraits of the legacies. The principal was explaining the history, and honestly, it was beautiful. The Santos line were men standing strong with the Santos sword passed down for generations. Each had a plaque with their victories I hadn't heard of. We finally made it to the trophy case. "We have several tournaments where everyone can showcase their talents. Everyone declares their abilities, we have a lot of first generations, but our legacies have suites, and each generation contributes a relic or victory. We look forward to seeing your abilities. We were on the 10th floor. This is the Santos Suite and your key. We trust it's to your liking. Orientation is tomorrow morning at 10." I smiled "Thank you Sir" The Principal smiled "I look forward to seeing your potential. Have a good rest."

The suite was amazing, 3 bedrooms 2 bathrooms, relics and portraits of my ancestors, furniture and items passed down through the centuries. My father is the last portrait. A giant library. I loved it. I was home. In the library, the Santos Crest was on the wall with two swords on either side. I sat at the large desk, reading through my schedule. I was taking "War Strategies, Hand to Hand Combat and a major in Politics." I went through my textbooks; I loved the smell of new books, and my schedule was amazing. My day started off crazy but for the first time since her, I genuinely smiled. But Willowdale had several more surprises for me and I couldn't wait.

Chapter 6
Willowdale.

Now call me a nerd. But Indiana Jones is my idol, and my biggest dream was to find the Ark of the Covenant. So finally sitting in that chair putting my fingers on the leather and wood on my fingers. My birthright. Now was my time. The Santos Heir. With complete control of my powers. The first thing I did was jump on the ladder and look for everything on the Ark. With my super speed that took a whole 10 mins, scanning through what my ancestors had potentially found. I was having the time of my life. "Henry" I called. Within 2 seconds he was in the room "Yes Miss, coffee? Tea. Lunch is already prepared." I smiled "Thank you Henry but I wanted to ask if the bike I requested had arrived?" Henry smiled "Yes Miss your Vincent Black Shadow arrived this morning, perfect for the narrow streets of Portugal" I grinned like a child "Thank You. Since Lunch is prepared why don't you take the night off, I plan to be exploring" I said excitedly "Thank You, Miss, I will ensure that you are ready for your orientation at 10. Have a pleasant evening" he said with a smile. Henry finished up and left. I took my pants off, got the whiskey flowing put the sound system on "Rock n Roll" and danced like I didn't care who was watching. Thank God for soundproofing. I could have whatever I wanted. I wanted adventure, I mean it's not like I have to worry about dying. So, I got to do whatever I wanted. So far it was.

1. The Arc of the Covenant
2. The staff of Aaron and Moses
3. The Library of Alexander
4. Atlantis

I was excited already. The easiest was Moses's staff, which was supposedly on display, but probably not real. Oh yes and a broom. I wanted to fly a broom. This is going to be epic. The sound stopped suddenly. "Really? Joan Jett?" I looked at Lu "Seriously? Ever heard of alone time?" Lu insisted on showing me around my campsite in my pouch which was covered with art and artifacts. He explained like was a tour guide " Most of the art and such were taken from Hitler, a few from Winston but he didn't care. Great guy. And now they are yours. You can officially say you're a collector. The sword I had dropped had made its way to the world "Excalibur" he laughed "Well I thought it was ironic; not like it wasn't built for ethnic cleansing" We laughed. Anyway, Michael. The stunt you pulled upstairs, a masterpiece by the way, kinda pissed him off and he's like the protector of Isreal or some shit. Nothing to worry about because we can't really kill each other but he is probably going to spout some self-righteous bullshit and start a fight so be on the lookout." He said nonchalantly. "I do enjoy a good fistfight." We bounced back to my office, and he looked around, not looking very interested. "Nice list," he said smirking. "I think so" I smirked back.

I was woken up again by Henry with breakfast in bed before orientation. "Miss..." Henry started "Your mother is furious." I looked at him drinking my vitamins "My mother is a narcissist" Henry looked nervous "She cut off the credit cards." I looked at him "Let me enjoy orientation and I will fix that after" He smiled unsure. He still didn't know.

Orientation started with the principal's speech "Welcome, all. Every one of you has been chosen for your abilities and some of you are descendants of the oldest bloodline. But be warned here at Willowdale you will encounter many things dragons, giants, creatures your wildest imagination couldn't conjure up. Willowdale is not a school. Willowdale is a test...and for some a prison."

We were divided up after that. Ice breakers, the Baine of my existence. " Shall we start with our names and powers" The oldest bloodlines had to wear capes. Just tradition. They sniggered at most if not everyone, they stank of privilege and mommy and daddy issues. When my turn came, I simply said, "I'm the Santos legacy, and I can feel emotions and control the energy in the room" Always play your cards close to your chest. I smiled and made sure to sound very girly.

On my way back my phone rang. It was my mother. I'd been avoiding this "Hi Mom" I answered "What the hell is wrong with you? Don't think because you're there, it's just one giant party. You may be the heir, but we control the purse strings! Remember that!" My mother had always been harsh she hated the idea of being a lesbian, not sure what I did this time, and she had no control other than money over me "No problem" I smiled into the phone "That's easily remedied" She hung up on me. Some things never change. Well, when shit hits the fan go home...then read a book.

The first thing that came to my mind. The 'Kruger Millions' is supposedly a hoard of gold hidden by President Paul Kruger during the South African Boer War. He tried to keep it out of the hands of the British. Estimated at $500 million. Finally, back at my suite, I pictured the president I was in the memory of Boers throwing the gold into a waterfall in Nelspruit. I smiled and snapped my fingers. Kruger coins filled the suite. Shit, that's a lot. "Henry!" I screamed. He came in and was automatically turned white "Well... Miss" he stuttered, and he looked as white as a ghost. I think I was starting to scare him. I looked at him and said, "Do what you usually do, that thing where I get interested each month" and with that, I walked into the library and carried on about my business. He had a look on his face that said, "This is madness."

About 4 hours later I came out for lunch, Henry handed me a black card. With my name on it. Not my parents. "You get half a million a month in return" Henry started and handed me documents and a black card. I scanned it. "Perfect. Thank You, Henry. I will put a debit order for your salary immediately." As I pulled out my phone I transferred him a $50000 bonus. "Thank you, Miss.," I smiled "Lunch is ready." He started "Perfect, please feel free to take the evening off. I wish to have some time to myself" He smiled "Of course Miss, Good Evening" Thank God Henry had his connections, and it would take me 2 seconds if he did try to scam me. I shook his hand, and I saw a man of his word. That was enough for me. This wasn't the first time my curiosity saved me, and I doubt it would be the last, but one thing was clear. All answers can be found in a library. For the first time, I had a chance to cry because I missed Charlotte. Someone willing to die for what was right. What did I want.......and what was right? The principal's words were being played over and over again. What was my next move?

I put on my leather jacket after I ate. I needed a long drive. I took the elevator down to the basement and admired the vintage beauty Vincent Black Shadow, the hum of the motor was like music to my ears. I put my helmet on and took off. This was exactly what I needed. Porto was beautiful. The energy was amazing. About 2 hours later I pulled back into the basement. It was dark and a swoosh pushed me off my bike. I was terrified I could feel the darkness. In front of me stood a woman in full pirdah. Blood dripping from her fingers. We stared at each other my chest was pushing back and forth as my breaths became deeper. Suddenly she surged forward lifting her arms grabbing my face with her bloody hands and promptly disappearing. Like dust flowing right through me. I shuddered, shaking and trying to press the button to my suit my face was covered in blood as looked at myself in the elevator's mirror. I needed a fucking drink. I grabbed a bottle of whiskey and shaking texted Lu "Did you feel that?" Lu replied instantly "It didn't come from my side. Might be Michael. But this came from the Muslims" Lu said "Jinns are not to be messed with. I'm trying to trace it, I'll come up as soon as I have something." I drank myself to sleep.

Needless to say, I was late for my first class. I put glasses on to hide the hangover. And tried to sneak in but the lecturer was not having it. Politics "Miss Santos!" He was old, musty, and grumpy "I see that we believe that rules don't apply to legacies. Rules exist for a reason. Take your undeserved seat but remember justice will catch up to us," he said dryly. Deep bruh. I didn't say anything and took my seat. Mr Assburger continued. "As I was saying..." There was a mugshot on the projector "This is Mr Connor McDowell, known child molester, currently responsible for raping and killing 37 children and counting. Holding him accountable has become a political issue as he crossed the border to Romania and the government refuses to get involved, our diplomats are currently negotiating, at the very least, a manhunt. If you open your textbooks to 334 to see the negotiating international law" The lecturer looked over his glasses "That being said, he is a very elusive character. He seems to possess an ability of invisibility and speed." He paused almost like it was for dramatic effect. The first person to bring him to me, if anyone, will be allowed to compete against the 4th years in hand-to-hand combat." I look through the textbook "I wouldn't worry too much Miss Santos; we don't expect much from you." He smiled a disgusting, smile "Well, Sir then I will get you'll 'much'" What a dick.

I went back to my suite where Henry had lunch ready for me, I sat at the table and looked at this guy's file. Graphic is not the word. I poured myself a glass of whiskey and lay out each victim that was brutally killed and raped, babies...children. The flashes again. My head exploded with a headache as I saw more flashes. This motherfucker was on a train. I got up jumping to the train. Right into his carriage. I sat opposite him and asked if he had a light. I lit up a cigarette and took a long pull while looking him dead in the eye. He broke the silence. "You can't smoke in here," He said calmly, I looked at him and giggled "This is Romania, isn't it? From what I heard you can do whatever the fuck you want." I tilted my head even giving a small smirk. Suddenly he looked very nervous and abruptly not to mention foolishly tried to run. He had climbed his way to the top of the train. I heard him run. I jumped up. Pulled up my sword and walked towards me. He looked terrified. I finally sped and grabbed his neck. Slowly I began to tighten and tighten. All with a smile on my face. Tighten. I could feel him wondering why I wasn't just killing him. Eventually, it was so tight his head fell off. I made sure to catch it. I opened a gate to hell and kicked whatever remained down. The hounds will enjoy that. I held his head by his hair and muttered "Fucker" I jumped into Mr Ass's class I put the head on his desk, I looked for a pin, I found a piece of matter and just wrote "Much?" and pined it to the fuckers forehead. Maybe it was a bit much, but I was worried that a woman may appear again if I didn't keep my mind busy. She wouldn't. She couldn't. Plus, Mr Ass wanted McDowell alive for something and now he's dead and I have his thoughts. Checkmate. Motherfucker.

I made my way back to my suite and Henry looked at me shocked "Good Evening, Miss" That's what I loved about Henry, he suspected but he never pried, and he never judged. Giving me my space. He was the only other person that cried when they dragged me away. My Grandfather. I have so much to grieve I didn't even know where to start.

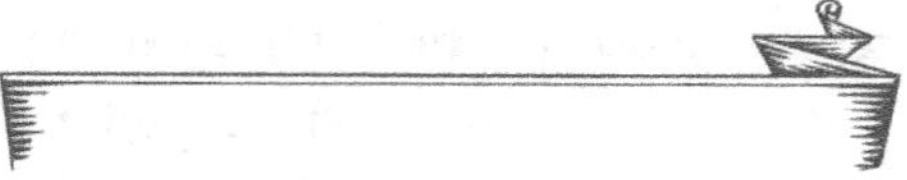

Chapter 7
Michael.

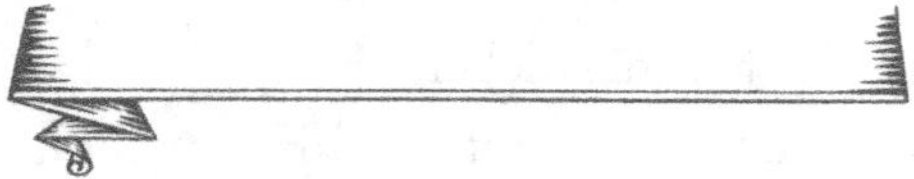

Mr Ass walked past me in the hall with a smug look on his face. Aww I could feel the humiliation he intended; He had set a beyond difficult spot test. I could not wait till he walked into his office. I bounced out of there. I wanted to see his face in class. My next class with him was only tomorrow. I attended War Strategies, and that lecturer seemed nice enough. It was mostly history, so I thoroughly enjoyed it. The implications on the battlefield: kinetic or firepower, mobility, protection and shock action, and the application of our abilities with the strategies. I walked out of my class with my book, picturing what a battle would look like and what I would do. Truth is I wasn't sure. With my textbook in hand and my cloak on. I felt very studious. My phone vibrated in my pocket.

"Come down for a drink?" sent Lu. I replied, "Give me 5 minutes". I headed up to the suite and changed quickly. I jumped down. The music was pumping, and the drinks were flowing." You're here!" Lu smiled and hugged me. He handed me a bottle of whiskey. He dragged me to the VIP lounge. We sat and he crossed his legs and leaned forwards and says, "Now Michael, maybe a royal, dry nail in my ass but I think doing drag in pirdah is a bit of a stretch."

That was one of the things I loved about Lu, we both knew small talk was absolute bullshit, we got right to the core of everything from niceties and the movement of his stool movement. It was weird. But we just got each other. I mean he wanted to be king, and I was gasping for air, but his parts fit mine. His ambition and my empathy balanced the scales perfectly. "I think it was one of my demons. Her." I was playing with my bottle "If it was her, she had every right to kill me. Lu saw the look in my eye "She could never be a demon" he gave it to me straight. "I need to ask you something" Lu filled up our glasses "What if I moved down here? The parties go for days, and I don't have to feel this demon so intensely. Lu's eyes softened yet he managed to see right through me. "It's not over you know. I didn't look up from my cup "There is nothing left. I will never love another woman, the way I loved her." Lu looked understanding. After a pause, he said, "I think your ridiculous intelligence has managed to overlook something staring you dead in the face." I laughed and looked like I was about to cry "We are anomalies. Heretic's. Sinners.!" I got louder but continued "People like us are fated to be defeated. There is no happy ending for people like us. The best we can hope for is getting to see Michael in pirdah" and slouched down on the bottle at my lips.

Lu looked at me worried, then he reached out his hand "You don't belong here" he said. There was no malice to his words. Almost crying, I took his hand. He had pulled me into a memory.

We are sitting on church pews at what looks like a wedding. I looked up and I was standing at the altar. A grey streak in my hair but I looked a little nervous then canon in D started to play and everybody stood up. I couldn't see who she was, but she was a picturesque bride, I looked back at myself, and I was beaming. Next to me, a teenager was smiling. He looked like a younger version of me. The one whispered to the other smiling "Mom and Mummy are finally doing it! It only took them like a decade" He giggled at me as I smiled. Before I could see anything else Lu pulled me out of the memory.

He looked at me poured us another drink and said "That's why as sinners, heretics, anomalies even if the fates themselves are against us, we live. We fight. Not because of us but for them. Even if we believe that we are nothing. We know that they are everything. That's why we fight. Bad is not meant to defeat good. Bad is meant to balance good. You give up now. You've lost them before you've even tried. You can't stay because you don't belong here" I went silent. Tears still falling. He was right. I knew he was right. It was a bad day, not a bad life. I looked at him "I get all of that?" Lu downed his drink "Duh" he poured us another. "Now Michael..." he continued. "About that..." I started "Isn't he your brother?" I asked. Lu's face turned sour "Unfortunately," he said. "So, can't you just call and ask?" I said obviously. He sarcastically "Yes and then we can have a drink and laugh about the old times. Like when he kicked me out of heaven" Just then I got a flash, it was gold of some kind. These headaches were intense. Lu touched my shoulder "You, ok?" Another flash of flying through the clouds at an impossible speed. I thought that on was going to make me pass out. I sat down. Pulled the bottle for another swig. "He's on his way" I looked at Lu. "Well, a showdown should be fun" We continued drinking, but he never came. Probably up to something. I jumped back and fell into my bed. Once again blackout drunk. I fell into a deep sleep.

I was awoken by the sounds of birds. "Odd," I thought, I opened my eyes and saw the sky, so I immediately sat up. I was in the garden and my bed was beneath a beautiful apple tree. I got out of bed and immediately saw I was I was naked. It was peaceful. I'm not sure where the bed went but stood taking in its beauty. She appeared. Under the apple tree. It was Her. She smiled at me. I immediately took her in my arms and hugged her, maybe a little too tight...something was wrong. I didn't feel her. She wasn't there. She was like a shell. She smiled at me and then picked an apple off the tree and offered it to me. Something was wrong. This shit was looking familiar, and I don't know who this woman was, but it wasn't her. "Thank you," I said with a smile "but I'm not hungry" She looked displeased and stepped back. I quickly uprooted the tree and Michael appeared. I threw the tree at him. And a celestial battle followed. He decked me in the nose. But I gave as good as I got rugby tackling him to the ground and landing fist after fist. The garden looked like a bomb hit it. Suddenly we heard a roaring sound even Michael looked up. The gates were closing. I left Michael laying there and ultra speed grabbed the tree, and I was out. Standing in the middle of a park but ass naked with an apple tree. I jumped back to the institute and hid the apple tree in my pouch. Properly soiling it creating a 'mini garden' for it. I took a packet of peas and put it on my face, I had a black eye. Shit. I was late for Politics again. On my way, I texted Lu "Found him. Text him and tell him we want to meet in the second circle."

I didn't even try to sneak in but by the looks on everybody's faces it was pretty bad "Sorry I'm late." Mr Ass watched his steps around me. There was no quiz, but he did ask to speak to me after class.

After the lesson, everybody started to clear out. I stopped at his desk "You wanted to see me, Sir?" He looked nervous and eventually just said "How did you do it?" I looked at him unbothered "Do what Sir?" he came forward frantically "There was a head on desk!" Again unbothered I replied "Because 'I'm Francesca fucking Santos and honestly, you're a complete dick, so I guess my answer is; I did it with absolute pleasure" I laughed "I know why you wanted him alive because you wanted information but I don't see how giving that information to you benefits me....so if you're done shitting your pants. I have a very large tree to see too and a pissed-off angel that needs to learn a lesson." I picked up my satchel and left. He stood there gobsmacked. Shit. That felt good.

Lu had replied, "What the fuck happened?" I sighed and texted back "Meet me at mine, bring a green witch" When I got back to the suite, Lu was looking at me expectantly with a witch that was looking around the place curiously. Lu looked at me expectantly. I quickly pulled up my pouch and the 3 of us made our way down the narrow stairs. It was clear the 'mini-ecosystem' I tried to create. They both stared in Awe but eventually Lu started laughing and I joined him. Its madness. Madness, I tell you. "You stole the tree from the Garden of Eden?" barely finishing his sentence because we were laughing so hard we were struggling to breathe Eventually Lu could say "Jesus Fuck Frankie, never a dull moment" I was still laughing "Well tell your brother to stop being an ass." I was hunched over trying to catch my breath "Can the green witch keep it alive?" The witch finally spoke up "Of course I can but I need an hour. This is a new one even for me." She got to work, and Lu and I sat at the bar. Pouring drink after drink. Amongst the frivolity I asked, "Did Michael respond?" Lu downing his drink "Yip tonight at 11, why the second circle?" I looked at him. "Because I want to finish my fistfight." It was obvious. Lu shook his head "Well, this should be good."

The witch finally spoke, "There seems to be something buried in the roots..." It was like she was speaking to herself. "Doesn't seem to be drawing energy from it" We both looked at her. I picked up the tree with one hand and tried to see what she meant, it looked like gold...Should I pull it out?" the witch replied "Yes but be mindful the roots have started to grow around it; somebody must have buried it at the base of the tree.... Don't destroy the roots!" she yelled. I carefully removed the box. The tree using its roots crawled back to the soil and planted itself. "I think it will live." I said dryly, the giant gold box was heavy, even for me." Thank you I told the witch" She looked at me "Anything to irritate Michael." And with a poof, she disappeared" I dropped the box and sarcastically said "Your brother seems like a great guy"

I had the Tree of Life growing in my bag, a gold box I didn't bother to open, and I was in the 2-second circle of hell in the middle of the fight club. No powers allowed. Just knuckles. Michael was getting it. But so was I, I'm pretty sure he bruised my ribs, it was sweaty and gritty. It was clear both of us were angry, for different reasons but it was working. Eventually, we were beating each other Lu, of all people, stopped it and jumped up to the gentlemen's lounge. "Really? You two are like children" We were both fuming. "She desecrated the Pearl Gates and stole the tree of life!" Michael yelled. I laughed "Well when you're being a dick, bad shit happens" Lu interjected "Look, we can't kill each other so maybe we just need to stay out of each other's hair."

I gave him a dirty look "Did God send you?" Michael matched my look "No." he clenched. "So, what do you want? If God wanted me dead, it would have happened already" Lu stopped me "Could you give us a minute?" he looked at me. I left and went to the bar and took a bottle. They spoke for a few minutes and Michael disappeared. "Cleaning up my mess?" I said into the bottle "Nope. I told him to fuck off back to Isreal" Lu said apathetically. "Isreal doesn't exist" I looked at him funny "In his mind it does" Lu took a sip of his drink. Something in me told me this wouldn't be my last encounter with Michael. I looked at Lu "That's the biggest bush I have ever seen." We laughed but everything hurt. I took some ice from the bar and continued drinking as Lu, and I laughed at Dumbass.

I needed a shower and DIY my injuries, I was covered in blood and sweat. That was epic. My bathroom was amazing. Completely black and the water came down from the ceiling. Blood and water went down the drain. I dried off. Lucky no cuts just in my mouth. Mostly just small cuts and bruises. What a day. I finally had the chance to try those fancy pajamas Henry bought me. Henry was responsible for literally anything. I wore the same outfit every day, he was a lot a few variants. It was a top and shorts that felt like silk. I got into bed and the feather and down felt like heaven. I took my tablets and anticipated a great night's sleep. Again, I was wrong. Once my head hit the pillow. I switched the lights off. The room was dark. My adrenaline was coming down. It would take a few minutes for me to fully relax. My eyes slowly started to close but I was frozen with fear. The lady in pirdah was standing at the end of the bed. Our eyes were locked for what seemed like hours but was only a split second. Blood dripping down her hand passed her sleeve. Again, she jumped forward towards me on the bed. This time letting out a high-frequency sound. That was enough to break the hold over me and shuffled to put the light on and she was gone. Like dust blowing away. "I guess it wasn't Michael" I muttered to myself.

Chapter 8
This Bitch

Just then the doorbell rang I got up. Covered in blood I answered the door. There stood a flirty, blonde girl, who looked like she belonged to a sorority. "Hi," she said twirling her hair and blowing out bubble gum. Harley Quinn. I was covered in blood and not the scariest one standing at that door. "We are having a party; we haven't seen you at a few and I thought I might convince you. "Convince me?" she ran her finger down my breasts "Convince you." She said with a naughty smile "Well then..." I said, "Convince me."

Within seconds she jumped into my arms and I was making out with her against the door. Dam her lips were soft. We started undressing each other and if I ever needed a reason to believe in God...it was her perfectly shaped breast. I focused on her neck and carried her to the couch where my mouth began to work its way down her body. Both hands on her breasts I smelt her scent. God, I missed that. I was so wet. I pinned her arms above her head as I kissed her. She started moaning and the harder I went. The louder she moaned. Maybe it's because it had been so long, but I wasn't being gentle at all. Leaving marks everywhere I could. When I finally reached her panties. I smelt her. Heavenly, I pulled her panties off with my mouth and she pushed her pelvis up wanting my tongue because her hands were still restrained, and she couldn't push my head down "Please...." she begged. Painfully slowly I liked her from the bottom to the top "Oh my god!" she was screaming My tongue found her clit. The furniture was shaking. While I was sucking her clit, I surprised her and pushed 2 fingers in. My tongue and fingers working in sync. The screaming was music to my ears. She showed her strength breaking my hold on her and pushing my back against the couch. I was still devouring her neck. She bit my ear and said, "Put in another one." I bit her lip and obliged. "I'm going to ride you till the couch breaks," she told me sternly staring me dead in the eye, I moaned "Fuck yeah" watching her boobs bounce up and down that fast, pure bliss. And so, the crescendo started, I used my powers to make the most intense, long orgasm. She fell on me both of us trying to catch our breath. I looked at her, still out of breath "What were you saying about a party?" we both laughed. "Is it true?" she looked up at me "About the head?" I laughed pulled her closer and kissed her sensually and slowly "I think you just found out" She laughed as she started to get dressed. "Tomorrow, 5, Kappa House" and with that she gave me a naughty smile and let herself out...and yes, I did look at her ass on the way out.

I remember making love to Her, but this was something else. This chick was point-blank fucking. Good God. I needed that.

I finally stood up and put on a big shirt. Pulled out a bowl and made Kellogg's, then I took a glass out getting ready to pour myself a glass of whiskey as I leaned on the counter. Lu suddenly appeared pouring a drink. Lu made himself a bowl "Fill the whiskey the top, I don't think you're ready for this." The flatscreen flashed on "And standing by hearing from people on the ground policemen, firemen..." I stopped eating and looked up. It was the Twin Towers. The newscaster continued "Trying to get everybody alive..." I looked at Lu "That's a lot of innocents" Lu poured me more whiskey. "Any leads?" Lu replied" Yes. You are very calm, and it smells like sex in here" Lu looked around. "I understand everything happens for a reason but if it's celestial interference then we are within our rights to step in. Call the club and tell them to prepare for refugees while we investigate" Lu looked at me surprised "What?" I asked eating "You're very calm." I giggled. "Trust me. I'm not."

I took Lu to the office and pulled down a map. He clicked. "What the actual fuck? Isreal. Really?" Lu looked back at me "He wouldn't... he couldn't" and carried on drinking "Michael is stepping straight into his destiny, namely destroying you...." I said sarcastically."

"Strange the sights are the Gaza strip and the west bank both near large bodies of water, curious, the army keeps such close surveillance on these areas." I continued. Lu looked at me in disbelief. "Not that water would be needed but the salt is a nice touch. Lu covered his mouth. Lu looked disoriented.

Lu looked at me "But why the Twin Towers? That's America" I pulled the bible from its place on the shelf "Because everyone needs a scapegoat...and funding. Between islamophobia, colonization, and Apartheid, just how hospitable do you think Palestine is going to be? Put starving people in the desert and kill off all their family then send an angel to test them?" Lu looked at me and said, "...the only reason would be why?" I looked at him. "That's where I'm stuck and hoping you can shed some light" "No I can't. I was a block of ice remember?"

I think, I opened a book the major sin was "inhospitable treatment of resident aliens and sojourners at its worst, through the sexual humiliation of rape if it's a boy it warrants genocide, if it's a girl, it's just another day.' Yip sounds about right" I looked at Lu "Is he feeling left out...? What is his end game? Or is he doing his duty as the guardian prince of Israel?" I ate "The area originally belonged to the Cainites and then the Ottomans," Lu said needing a minute. So, I filled his drink. He looked up at me and I could see he had an idea "Why don't we just ask Cain?"

We jumped down. Cain was getting the hell beaten out of his by the minotaur. I screamed "Hey! I need a second with him." The guards brought him to us and kicked him to his knees. "Ok dude, what the fuck did you do on that land?" He looked down "I killed my brother." I rolled my eyes "We know that part. What else happened? Why does everyone want it?"

He looked defeated "The Arc of the Covenant, everyone thinks it's hidden under Al-Aqsa Mosque" Lu and I looked at each other comically "The mosque?" he repeated "Nope" from me," nah" from Lu. Cain looked shocked "Hey don't look at us like that brother killer" He looked down "The thing with the gold top," he said quickly "OOOH" Lu, and I said together "Yes that one. The Jews are convinced it's hidden under there. They need it for a ritual they want to take over." I interjected "Would you really need a ritual for that? They have most of Palestine now?" he looked at me stoically "Not Palestine they want to rid the world of all heretics" I looked at him "So basically anyone that doesn't believe what they believe? Isn't it true that Satan doesn't exist in the Torah?" Cain looked at me. Lu went completely silent. "What ritual exactly?" Cain laughed to himself "Black magic, my brother's bones, and his wife's rib, seeing as that was how women were made, I sort to eradicate them as well." I looked at him "You are the reason we can't have nice things" he laughed "You would need the witch..." I interjected "The witch?" he looked at me "Lillith, 3 pure red heifers, descends of Lut and the arch." Lu and I looked at each other "Where's the arch?" I asked "Lost somewhere in history, the Ethiopians have claimed they have it, but with no proof" I kicked him in his face "Take him, we're done" he grabbed onto my feet and said "You will need hundreds of thousands of men to even make a dent" He laughed. I grabbed him by his hair and laughed "My darling you may need those men, but Lu only needs one lesbian." I laughed and kicked him back to the second circle.

I looked at Lu, I know exactly what's going to cheer you up!" He looked at me "Fuck!" I followed him to the bar "Don't stress. Is it a lot of work? Yes. Am I going to kick his ass again? Also, yes. How bad could Ethiopia be?" Lu laughed "This motherfucker is going for gold" he continued "Shall we raise hell?" I smiled "Fuck yeah! Let's do this!"

"Where are you taking me?" I had his eyes closed with my hands "Trust me, it's heaven." We were standing in front of Kappa. "Surprise!" I removed my hands. Lu looked and realized, we looked at each other and screamed excitedly "Sororities Girls." And that is how the party started, amazing music, making out with random girls. Lu was busy feeling up a Senior while two girls dragged me upstairs. I held up my bottle of bourbon "I LOVE SORORITIES!!!!!" and I got an equally enthusiastic "FUCK YEAH!!!!"

Eventually, we found a room. Both girls started kissing my neck. Guess word got around. I took control. I frenched the sexy girl in yellow threw her on the bed and pulled her panties off under her cheerleading uniform while grabbing the other girl and kissing her passionately as I bit her lower lip, I turned her around and pulled her close so I could smell her hair. Fuck this was sexy. I pushed her mouth down to the other girl's pussy and slipped 3 fingers in, I was fucking her like this would be my last night on earth. Back and forth. Back and forth. I kissed her down her spine and made sure to mold her breasts from the back, pulling her nipples. Their moaning filled the air. I made sure to keep the pace while holding her head against the other girl's pussy. 2 hours later, I used my emotions to prolong their orgasms. The best part was hearing them moan. God, I love women. They fell onto each other. I seductively smiled "Thanks, ladies."

As I turned around. A hallucination, the desert, and the woman in pirdah her hands covered in blood, kneeling over a child with bullet holes over his body. She let out a high-pitched, bone-chilling screech. Suddenly I was back at the party. Lu looking at me "Are you ok?." I was covered in blood again. Yeah, I lied. "Come on, we have one more stop."

I led Lu to a small chapel. It was beautiful. Stained glass covered most of the building, built in 1907 and it only had pews for 15 people and a small altar. A few statues of the saints. It was the most peaceful place on earth. I told Lu to button up. I also pulled myself together trying to hide the blood. Nervously I knocked. I could immediately hear movement. A nun answered the door "Good Evening Mother Superior. Apologies for bothering you at this hour" She smiled, and I felt like I was that little girl again. Spending every break in the Chapel. "Francesca!" she smiled. She led us to the chapel through the library. I stopped and asked Lu if he wanted to wait in the library. Mother Superior and I did the sign of the cross and sat in the Chapel. She smiled at me "I knew this day would come" I looked confused "I used to see you during the break, praying and I used to think 'God please show her, her path because I see the warrior spirit in her'" she could see the tears in my eyes. "And here you are. I guess it's coming" I had to compose myself "Sister, I have so much pain and most days I feel broken. There's so much anger." She started choking up "You need to forgive my child, anger may be the obvious protection, but have you tried any other emotion, you know that you do have more than one?" she smiled and giggled "I'm proud of you my child. But you never go to war with somebody else's sword" The altar lit up and the marble moved in sync and in the middle stood a sword "I looked over at Mother Superior "Claim who are my child" I bowed before the altar and pulled the sword out. As I pulled it out, I could see and feel the electricity running through my veins. I held it up in awe. "It can't be seen by anyone but a few" I put it on my belt "Go well my child" We exited the chapel where Lu was pretending to be curious about the books "Thank You Mother Superior" I hugged her. We were walking out. "And Santos, do me a favour and don't die" I laughed "I will definitely try not to."

We walked out and it started to rain. Lu seemed unsure. "Everything Ok?" I replied "Yeah, I think it is. I need a nap though. Let's jump home and we can regroup tomorrow morning" I was back at the suite Henry had left my favorite comfort food cover on the table. I looked at the sword, it was beautiful. It almost looked like glass. I took the stairs down my pouch and put it on the wall with the one Lu gave me. I knew it would be safe, and I would know when I needed it. I was back upstairs in bed, out of the bloody clothes, and eating a mince, cheese with my favorite noodles made kinda like a stew. It was the best. I felt relaxed and slowly fell off to sleep. I was without a doubt sleeping late. Hand-to-hand combat tomorrow.

Chapter 9
Trials, lies and Lillith.

✕

"OH MY GOD!" HER FINGERS gripped the sheets "Yes! Just like that!" my tongue moved faster. God women are delicious. "I'm coming! I'm coming" her back arched in the sexist way as I felt the pulses of orgasm following through her. There was a banging at the door. Doof Doof Doof. "Sister Eunice, are you alright?" I quickly grabbed my clothes and bolted out the window "Yes.... I'm just feeling the holy spirit "I heard her say as I balanced on the roof tiles.

Balance wasn't my strong point. A personal day probably wasn't a good idea. Jumped to my bike on the street. Put on my leather jacket and sunglasses and sped through the traffic back to Willowdale. I pulled up and everyone was lingering outside. I forgot it was 'The Trial,' everyone speculating on who would be chosen, which trial it was, and if they would survive. I left before I saw anything and headed upstairs to change. Suddenly I was being pulled into a closet being kissed by a girl I had met at the party. I carried on kissing her and grabbed her ass.

The next thing I knew my head was on fire. Flashes of women in scarves. I crouched down "Terrorist!" and he spat. I recognized him. Was the pain I was feeling happening at the same time as the incident? That meant I could jump. I got up. Passionately kissed the girl and left saying "We can continue this later; I have to sort something out" Not giving her a chance to respond I gave her another kiss. I walked down to the 'The Games' and I saw the situation unfold in front of my eyes. "No way," I thought. "The girl with the scarf fell to the floor. "Should be easy for your kind, you like to blow things up." I didn't say anything. This trial would be the hardest one yet and I was pretty sure she was a first-year. She was crying. Mr Ass went to the microphone "Then it's settled Fatima Bhamjee will face this trial" God he was a dick. I spoke up "But Sir I thought you said that whoever passes your test can compete." I paused "I did give you a heads up" I wanted to laugh at how awkward he looked "Very well, you can die with her." I smirked. Don't get me wrong the Quran is possibly the most beautiful poem ever written to humanity. But I had run into Islamic communities before, the biggest mistake you can make is to read the Quran and then start socializing. It was a stark contrast to the depth of the Quran. It was self-involved programmed robots. Basically, bitches looking for husbands. I had never seen such selfishness up close, sometimes I wondered if they even had skin over their faces but 9/11 was a crime against humanity and they were way too self-involved to pull that off. But oh, did their words cut. A colosseum erupted up through the football field with us at the center. The rest of the school was bustling getting to their seats, buying popcorn gleefully waiting for us to die. I pulled her "Woman Up. We need to choose our weapons" I threw a sword at her, and she couldn't catch it. "Right. I will use the sword, and you stay behind the shield as much as you can. I strapped the shield to her arm. She had tears in her eyes but now she just looked scared. "Stay behind me and I will make sure you survive.... just remember Up" It seemed the Rector was to give a speech "Welcome all to the first trial of the season!" Everyone cheered "These are the most dangerous events any warrior will encounter and prove their abilities!" Another cheer "But most importantly it will determine your destiny." Everybody cheered. Settling down once the rector took his seat. I didn't know what to expect. I closed my eyes, and my shadows appeared. They looked ready for war. "We've got you" Mr. Ass announced, "The first trial: An army of 20 of our strongest warriors." More cheering. I called the sword Lu had gifted me. I had a feeling this will be fun. I looked over at the girl "hide in the trench and cover yourself with the shield" I touched the shield; she's got about 4 hours of invisibility.

Now these dumbasses. I could make it quick, or I could enjoy myself. They all came running towards me, the sweat, the anger, and the sheer stupidity. It was clear to me this was a waste of my time. I took out my sword, closed my eyes, and with one vertical slash from my sword, the ground started to open where I imagined. Each warrior runs straight into the fault. Running in a straight line...well he did say the strongest, not the smartest. With the last warrior hanging on the fault closed. The was very underwhelming. "I thought this would be more exciting." I pulled Fathima out of the trench, she figured no one could see her. "Go home," I said softly.

Suddenly everyone went silent. "Anything else?" I asked as if everything was completely normal. Everyone's mouth was open. The rector eventually cleared his throat "Our Winners Fathima Bhamjee and Francesca Santos" No one knew how to respond to that. "Well if that's all..." I spoke. "It's not..." a tall thin man in a grey thobe stepped forward. "Right....and how can I help you?" I didn't mind honestly. Not like the trial was a challenge. "Well, it has come to my attention, that you and I will have a dual...very soon." I looked at him "Did you want to start early?" he chuckled. "No...just seeing my competition" and with that, he disappeared. Wow. I wasn't going to get to do any hand-to-hand combat today. But a pick-me-up came to my rescue. Loud music blearing ACDC pulled up. "Get in. We have a lead" I looked at everybody still silent, and I awkwardly said "Thanks guys, this was fun. That's my ride. We should do it again sometime" I jumped at the back of his open Jeep and was ready for some real fighting "Let's do this bitch!" and Lu recklessly pulled off and hit an old forgotten road. Ethiopia here we come! Flashing through space the jeep landed in Ethiopia. We were in front of the Church of Our Lady Mary of Zion, where the Arc was claimed to be "Lu got out of the Jeep and I jumped off. "So..." I asked "How do you want to do this? Guns blazing or peacefully?" Lu chuckled "You honestly think they're going to give up the arc peacefully?" I laughed "True. Well then let's do this" I sent out a massive pulse and the doors blew open. I didn't waste any time. I looked at who seemed to be the priest and said, "Where is it?" Everyone looked scared but it's not like we would ever hurt civilians. But they didn't know that. The priest lifted his crucifix, his hand shaking "In the name of Jesus, I rebuke you…" Well, this is awkward. "Yeah, Jesus can't come to the phone right now." And with that I grabbed both sides of his head, searching. Wow, that was easy. I looked at him "Is there any woman you haven't slept with?" Lu laughed. "In the basement" I looked at Lu. By dinner time we had a gold box on the table and stuffing our faces with the buffet Henry had prepared for us. It was a long day. We even made the news, watching as the Priest recounted about the demons that had infiltrated the church. We could not stop laughing. I nearly choked. Then after some time. We went quiet. I looked at Lu "So? Shall we?" We were both on either side "1,2,3" and we lifted the incredibly heavy gold lid. We both looked inside. "Ok so a rock, I'm assuming is the Ten Commandments a staff, I'm gonna assume is the staff of Aaron." I looked at Lu "There's no way to know if this shit is real or not" Then we both got the fright of our lives "Oh it's real." I stepped back "The fuck?" She smiled, now normally I would love to have a sexy woman in my suite. "Lillith" she smirked "Oh, that makes sense," I said. "We have some questions if you don't mind. I mean I think we did just free you." She smirked "As long as you have whiskey." I smirked back "Shall we move to the parlor?" She smiled and walked past Lu "Lucifer" she greeted "Lillith" he said back, but I couldn't read his expression, and I was feeling apprehension. We shared a look, and I followed. I looked at him and shared an emotional thought, it said "Relax, worse case we put her back in the box."

I don't know if it was an energy that picked up in the room but as Lu handed me a glass of whiskey, time showed as the glass fell, and my full powers were activated. The shadow appeared immediately and said "Put her back. Now" Pulses were radiating from my hands, and I grabbed, she screamed out in agony "What happened to…" trying to get the words out "… a civil conversation…" I ignored her and pushed even more anger through my pulses "Where are the bones?" She gasped "The last time…I saw it Enoch was burying it by a tree…that's all I know" she cried out in pain "That's all I know!" she begged as if she knew we were going to put back. Lu didn't miss a beat he grabbed her while I pushed her in with my pulses. Once she is in. He closed the box. "Sweet baby Jesus." Lu looked and relieved "What a day." I sat, I grabbed a bottle of whiskey "So I'm guessing there's a story there." I was beyond tired. "Well..." Lu started as he grabbed a bottle and threw himself next to me "Let's just say she is the literal ex from hell." We laughed tiredly "Tomorrow is another day, and I think we should have opened that box we found under the tree of life...we will check it out tomorrow." I yawned. "Thank you," Lu said stoically. My eyes were closed but I was still sipping "For what?" I said not opening my eyes "I've never had a friend." Now I opened my eyes. "Well, aren't bad at it either. So, thank you to...I guess" There was a pause. A silence. "Ewwh." I let out "Yeah, no emotions suck" Lu added our faces looking like we just ate something sour.

The next day we opened the box, "A box of pure gold with bones inside." Lu laughed "What are we going to do it?" Lu looked unfazed "I dunno, just keep it here" I looked at him as we headed back up "Disaster averted. Now I have to get back to college". Lu laughed at me "What could they possibly teach you? You found the Arc of the Covenant?" I sighed "It's more of a formality." Lu laughed and jumped not before saying "Out loser."

I put on my cloak and went down the elevator, I needed to buy food as Henry was off today. I strolled into the food court; it was like the air had been sucked out when I walked in. I scared them. I carried on as normal and grabbed a tray, investigating what was for lunch" ...spaghetti and meatballs.... hmmm lasagne" I thought. I finally decided on Lasagne with a garlic roll and side salad and a cool drink. I walked up to the checker, and smiled "Hi, how are you doing today" he seemed aback "Good...that will be $55 please". I placed a hundred on the counter and smiled "Keep the change" he looked down and his mouth fell open "Thank you" he smiled as looked around where to sit. The whole looked like they were holding their breath. I scanned the room. I wanted to be alone. I saw an empty table in the corner and got comfy. I took out some light reading Blaming the victims. It was a set book for War Strategies. I blocked out the world as I read and ate, and slowly people started murmuring and talking again. All was well for now. 'OH yeah, I thought, Mr Ass tried to kill me yesterday.' I giggled to myself; he's probably shitting himself right now. It felt very therapeutic. Sitting, reading, and eating. But reality does come knocking. Ninja Phirdah was still doing her thing. At some point, I must sort that out. She was standing at the end of the cafeteria near the door blood on her hands. I didn't flinch this time. I just looked at her. She stared as if she was staring into my soul.

The stare was broken by the girl from yesterday "Hello" she repeated herself. I finally came back to reality "Yes, Hi what's up?" She looked at me as if she expected some response. Eventually, I was just like "What" I could see on her face she worked up but thrilled "Ummm you put the army to shame, and you saved me yesterday? Like, hello?? Do you realize what this means?" My face scrunched "What?" she scoffed "Umm you're pretty much the most powerful one here, you could claim the champion's sword and own this place?" I was indifferent and grabbed a piece of garlic bread "Yeah...I have enough swords." I had no interest in seeking power within Willowdale, that's like being a prefect and a kiss ass plus I had a lot of shit on my plate right now, and I didn't have time for childish trials. I mean for god's sake I survived being tied to a pole for 3 days, all the elements, and no food or water. I had nothing to prove "Are you crazy?" I looked at her "Listen I know I helped you out yesterday, but we are not friends. Me not wanting you to die is not the same as having a friendship" Her face fell. I preferred to be honest and not waste her time. "Plus, I don't like bullies." She walked away frustrated, and I carried on eating my lasagna which wasn't bad at all. I wiped my mouth and packed up. Mr Ass would be waiting. It's weird, I suddenly had this feeling that fate was bending towards where it should be. "Gawr As Safi is the city that borders both the Dead Sea and Isreal or Palestine depending on your stance it currently is home to sugar cane fields Museum at the Lowest Place on Earth containing the Sanctuary of Lot. If the Israeli military were to invade, they would be met with cow herders and small villages. There would be little to no resistance." I listened, I remembered the story of Lut and his wife that turned into a pillar of salt but mostly I was thinking about all this talk about invasion.

Chapter 10
True power is silent.

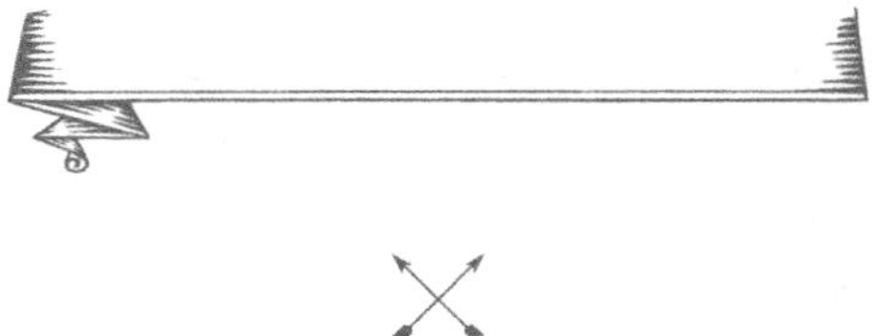

A FEW DAYS PASSED, and I started making a habit of eating in the cafeteria and reading, it was fun. One day, which I'm assuming, this dumbass was feeling particularly brave, pulled the book out of my hand. It was the dumbass that spat at the girl with the scarves "My, my...what do we have here?" I looked at him "I'd tell you to read but I think there are a few words you can't pronounce." His face turned red, and his nostrils began to flair "It would take me a second to snap your neck. So, I suggest you put my book down and walk away." I said calmly. His face changed very quickly. He put the book down and walked away. 'Dumbass' I thought.

I carried on reading, but I needed to go to the library about the Dead Sea and maybe even speak to Lut I'm pretty sure he impregnated all his daughters. Also, what the fuck is up with Aaron and cows and shit. And I'm the fucking sinner? A gust of wind opened the book on the following page. I carried on reading. But it seems that Aaron's staff and that giant rock have celestial power. What's with the aroma situation? They do know everything is covered in blood. I thought apathetically and then right after 'This is why you would be burned about at the stake.' I closed the book and headed to my suite. I thought I was finally going to get a break I heard screeching from an old school microphone. "Hello Willowdale!!!! After an exciting first trial, everyone waiting with bated breath to see what the next challenge will be!! Only gets harder from here! Good Luck to Fathima Bhamjee and Francesco Santos!!!!!" He said enthusiastically .... wait what? Just then Fathima ran up to me "Do you get it now?" I was honestly annoyed we did it once, what else did they want? "What shit is this now?" I said to her rather abruptly. "There are five trials genius. We only survived the one" I looked at her annoyed "What's the next one? You know what let's just go to my suite and we can see how the hell we can get out of this" I walked past her to the elevator, and she followed. Once we were in my suite she looked around curiously while I went straight to the bar. Whiskey makes everything better. She looked unimpressed

"You know I'm a Muslim right?" My eyebrow rose. "Your point being?" I said disinterested "Muslims don't drink." She said sternly. "I didn't offer…" I say unbothered "and at least I don't have to share."

She sat down with a stern look on her face. "Why did you help me? You hate Islam. Was it just an opportunity to prove your power" I scoffed as I downed my drink and filled another glass, making sure there was extra. "You are wrong on so many levels. Islam has shown invaluable lessons. It opened my eyes to the world." I said seriously. "A label is just a label." I nursed my drink. "Islam, the bible, Torah. Call it what you want. That's what got me here…alive…feeling like shit but alive" I stared off into the distance "It took everything I loved, the only thing I loved. But I'm alive." She had a straight face. "Allah has a plan for everyone. What is meant to happen, does. What are you going to tell me next? God isn't real?" I laughed into my glass almost spilling it. I could she was getting angry "God. Heaven. Hell. Does exist." I looked her dead in the eye "I can say that because I was there." My response surprised her. I sat back crossed my legs and took another sip. I looked at her "What? You're surprised?" She looked gobsmacked. "I looked selfish straight into the face while they dragged her away and killed her. Molina's holding me down so I couldn't do anything. Islam is selfish, an excuse for hurting one another, and the only reason for charity is for rewards at the end. I wonder what reward they got for killing her. As for the Christians, they had no problem killing someone trying to save me. I held as bleed out through the bullet hole in her throat." I moved my eyes from the fire back to her, "It doesn't work like that." She said quietly. I smiled "Right and flying planes into civilian territory is acceptable according to everyone because it's Allah's will? The Taliban got their message across, Bush is going to declare war and become president again ahh don't you just love politics! Businesses will make billions from weapons and surgical supplies. And I know for a fact it wasn't the Devil because he was with me at the time. None of this is about religion. None of this is justice. The label doesn't matter.

It's staring us dead in the face but no one will admit it because we are inherently selfish, call it what you want, religion, politics, patriotism. It's all just greed" She leaned forward "How do you know this?" I laughed. "I died like twice, I think. Don't stress I ended up in hell, I just had a difference of opinion at the gates of heaven with Peter." Her mouth fell open.

As if exactly on time Lu jumped in "Frankie...blue or black?" He held two ties up. "We are on high alert." He said seriously. I laughed and looked at him "You mean you have a date?" He looked scared. "Black, it's more elegant...relax just pretend it's you and me and talking and just be honest." Lu looked at my guest "Oh Lucifer this Fatima, we are doing this trial shit together." He took a deep breath "I've got this." I looked at him confidently "You've got this." He jumped and I sat across from Fatima again. I looked at her "Now I answered your questions, answer mine." Fatima took a deep breath "I'm assuming you have an idea about this task? And an invasion is imminent?" She took off her scarf and poured herself a drink. "Bold," I said impressed "I'm from Gawr As Safi and in the next few days blood will be shed." I looked at her and downed my drink "The Americans are going to Afghanistan? How do you know?" I looked at her. "I'm a seer. I saw you coming and I know there's a woman in Pirdah with bloody hands trying to get hold of you." This surprised me "She's trying too maybe." I looked at her with a neutral face "I'm failing to see how this is my problem, I'm an anomaly none of this affects me?" "The city borders both the Dead Sea and Palestine, they are using illusion to take over the Holy Land again. The Americans will create such a campaign, it would overshadow crossing a border with no safety on Jordans' side and ultimately with American support and this army they can take back the holy lands." She was working herself up. "Still fail to see why this is my problem?" She was getting frustrated "That is the trial. And if you don't fight. I will fight alone" She looked adamant "You are a 1st year...and a seer. What exactly are you going to do?" I smirked "Best advice I can give you. Stay out of it. This is not our war." She looked desperate. "I can pay you, name your price." I filled both our drinks "Money means nothing." She drank more and "Gold, women, anything..." as she went on. The TV flashed on. The newscaster broadcasting from Jordan "I'm here in Jordan, where locals will go back to sleep in a panic, some have even packed as much as they can, to move further from the border, this was all triggered by an unknown army build-up, in Palestine across the board." The newscaster held her ear "We just got an update, breaking news, that Princess Salma has been taken hostage." My neck slowly rose. I pulled my phone out and googled 'Princess Salma.' I froze. My blood turning cold. It was her. It was Her. She's alive.

I forgot about everything else and jumped to the border. I immediately went up to some locals and told them to evacuate. I held my hand to my chest. We may not all understand each other's languages. But a Warrior's spirit recognizes another.

Once I had decent space between civilians and the army. The army looked at me and laughed. I. Really. Don't. Like. Bullies. I bent down on my knee, took out my pocketknife, and cut a line on the palm of my hands, I let the blood drip to the ground walked over to the water, and put a few drops in. It was still nightfall. I heard a phone ring and a soldier saying "Yes, they have a short, fat girl monitoring the border. Once the order has been given it should take maybe 2 seconds?" I walked to the gate "Good Evening, Officer" I took the phone from his hand "Hi there dipshit. Listen I'm going to need Princess Salma back otherwise in 2 hours, I will kill everyone under your command. My team will kill, burn, and destroy anything and everything in sight. Then a tiny penis will destroy the holy land, you like radiation, don't you? So, no one will claim, not to mention I know where the arc is. You have two hours to comply with. I demand proof that she is safe, or I will kill all of you anyway...." I smiled "Just remember if you ignore me, I won't kill you, I will make you wish for death."

I sat on the sand, running my fingers through the sand as it mixed with my blood. Ancestral power. I feel could a few powerful pulses. I could change the entire landscape if I wanted. I laid down absorbing the power. Checking my watch every so often. See? This is why you only need 1 outfit. I had to get up. A man was approaching; I think he came to find out if I was Taliban. I used my memories, I took his hand and let him see. He had also come to drop off some food. The memory made him smile and he couldn't stop thanking me. I felt bad. I was being selfish. I'm only here for her. Perhaps there is a way to ensure the protection of the innocent. I was back in the sand recharging. I will not let her slip through my fingers again.

About an hour later a tall thin man in a grey thobe stepped forward. I recognized him. He was the one at the Colosseum, talking about dual. He walked with power and confidence. I stood up from rolling in the sand "I know you, you're the dual guy" His jaw clenched, "I would ask why you're here, but I think we both know. I am Prince Ahmed" I looked at him "Plus I've given my demands. Duh. What exactly are you the prince of or did you just give yourself that title because you kidnapped the Princess?" I stopped "I'm assuming you're here to agree to my terms." He gave a condescending chuckle "Pulling off 1 trick in a child's game doesn't make you ready for war. You're alone. You have no army, my snipers can take you out in 3 seconds, and you have the nerve to ask about the Princess." I suddenly realized that if I could project emotions maybe I could project consequences. "The Princess is to be my bride. She will be treated as such" I smiled "Well whoever lays a finger on her will have their dicks fall off." His smile quickly turned to anger "And I like the big talk about marrying. Islamically that's her choice. Plus, it doesn't matter what you want. She's coming home with me." I stated factually. If looks could kill. I would die looked at his face "You don't even have an army." I giggled "Who said I don't have an army?" He stomped his foot "Fine then embarrass yourself!" I immediately let out a powerful pulse that rendered every mechanical weapon useless.

His workers began setting up highchairs so that he could watch, that's when I finally caught sight of her, our eyes connected and I felt more whole as if the broken pieces of my soul had been put back together. She sat next to him, with guards behind them. Before them was an army filled with inbreeds on camels, elephants, and horses. He had a smug look on his face. I saw him force her to take his hand.

'Well,' I thought 'game time.' I kneeled on one knee again and closed my eyes making sure to rub sand on my hands again. I stood. They were maybe 7km from me. I couldn't think of anything as this army was torpedoing towards me. My safe song "Imagine" by John Lennon, fun fact, music releases pulses, and slowly the ground started to shake, and I carried on singing with every emotion I had. Our ancestors started to climb out covered in ash and pissed as hell, even hissing; the people of Lut. If I'm being honest if they find him and kill him, I will look in the opposite direction, that guy is a dick. Soon it was clear my army was bigger than his and because were close to the Dead Sea thousands more came, Including a giant ship ready for battle. Each one came of them and stood behind me.

I turned to look forward and I saw Pegasus. I rubbed his head, there was a note on the saddle "On loan. xoxo Lu" He is so lame. I mounted Pegasus and flew over the armies landing in the middle. "Ancestors, I stand here before you as a depravity, a mistake, an anomaly. History has not been good to us, the sick, the different, the witches, the adulterers, the homosexuals, the prostitutes. They judged and punished people like us and what right do they have?" The crowd yelled and the clanking of the army filled the air "If we are different then we are condemned!" More yelling "And for what? Love? Herbs? Enjoying a full moon? Wanting to read? Accusing us of famine, disasters, and disease? They have already sent us to hell! What more can they do" I paused. I lifted my sword into the air "NO MORE" I started screaming "NO

MORE!" was chanted till we met in battle two seas of living and dead clashing. The energy of justice was intoxicating. I made Pegasus follow me above as I rolled off into the middle of the action. Immediately sliced a running soldier on the knee as I made my way to her. It was a bloodbath, but no blood was shed on our side.

A soldier decided to wield his sword at my head. I blocked him with my arm and stabbed her on the side of him in the throat. I was getting close to Salma. I heard the guard say in Arabic "We should kill her now. We are losing" Within seconds I had sliced a soldier's throat and taken his bow. The princess calmly said "I wouldn't try anything" Salma said with a knowing look. She knew me too well because as she said that an arrow went straight through his eye pinning him to the wall. When I finally got to Salma the guards tried to stop me. I incinerated each one of them with pure anger. Now that there was no barrier. I asked, "What kind of man allows his people to shed blood for him while he refuses to shed his own?" I whistled for Pegasus as he ran for his horse. I grabbed her and put her on Pegasus. "Take her to the palace." I smacked his butt. He sneered at me "Are you going to kill me?" I laughed. "No..." I stared into his soul, and he ran to his horse and abandoned what little army he had left.

I walked through the war area that was now a graveyard. I had a plan. In the middle of the field. Making sure I targeted the fault system; I summoned every feeling of hate and anger that could and pulsated such a concentrated wave of power. The ground parted and inside all you could see was brimstone. The ancestors dragged the bodies of the dead back to the opening and if anybody were to try to attack this village. They would have to go through hell. I took the last of my energy, letting out a pulse of gratefulness. I held my hand to my chest and the army and villager did the same.

Chapter 11
Got Milk?

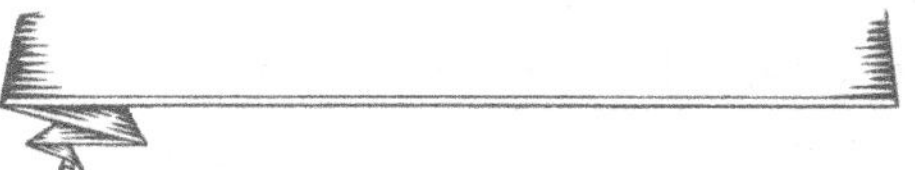

I was once again covered in blood, and I still had my armor on. I jumped to a bush near the palace. Climbed down the stairs in my pouch and took a nice hot shower. The adrenaline was wearing off and I could feel the tiredness in my bones. This pouch was the best gift I have ever been given. I threw myself on the puffy bed feeling refreshed yet tired and at some point, I fell asleep, at one point I woke up groggy to see that Pegasus was sleeping at the end of the bed and then I fell back to sleep. Eventually, I woke up, took a shower, and tried to make myself presentable. Which just means I had a different shade of t-shirt on, jeans, and vans. Pegasus came out with as I closed my pouch. And we flew to the castle door.

I knocked but nobody answered. So naturally I kicked them down. "I know I'm late," I straightened up "I have come to ask for Princess Salma's hand in marriage." The Moulana came forward "I'm afraid Prince Ahmed has already offered mahr" I smiled "Then surely I can counter his offer or at the very least let the Princess accept or decline?" The Moulana didn't argue but made his way to the chambers on the side of the hall. While we waited, I whispered "So you're a Prince? Now I can call you PP. The Pussy Prince" I laughed to myself and fiddled, it was clear who was tense and who wasn't. The Moulana came out "The Princess has asked what the offers are?" A royal from PP's side came forward "The Prince would like to offer "50 million dollars in gold bars" Two strong men came forward with a chest containing gold and jewels" The Moulana looked at me. "To have the Princess on my arm would be priceless therefore I ask her to name her to name her price" The Moulana went back to the chambers "The Princess had requested 3 red heifers without defect or blemish and that had never been under a yoke. Their heads will suffice." Romantic. "I, Prince Ahmed will prove myself..." I rolled my eyes "Oh shut the fuck up" I knew where the Israelis were hiding them. I jumped, I sliced 1,2,3 and I jumped back "The princess's wishes will always be fulfilled." I declared wholeheartedly. The Moulana smiled and proceeded to the chambers.

"PP" I kept whispering and laughing. The Moulana smiled. "Miss Santos, the Princess accepts your mahr. You may wait in the parlor till she is ready for you. Prince Ahmed, you are free to leave." I laughed "Bye PP" He left with his tail between his legs like the little bitch he was. "You do realize I'm a millionaire, right?" He sneered at me. I giggled at that; I keep track of my finances in my email. I was close to 800 million dollars. Not like I spend much. But I had nothing to prove. I had already won. So, I smiled.

I was led into the parlor to wait. My phone rang. It was Lu so I picked up quickly "Whoop, what a night! You smashed, I smashed. Epic does not even begin to describe this." I giggled softly "Look dude, I can't talk tonight but I will call as soon as I can. Lu responded with "Get it Gurl!" I could hear him snapping his fingers on the other end. I just put the phone down and put it on silent.

The shadows appeared "If you're here to yell at me, I don't have time right now." They smiled "Somebody wanted to speak to you..." they parted and there stood my grandfather. I immediately started crying and ran into my arms "My baby, I am so proud of you" I just sobbed. "Please stay" He smiled "I love you, remember that" and they just faded away. I was alone again.

I waited about 15 minutes then the Moulana came to get me. He led me to a large golden door "Just knock, congratulations on your union" he smiled and disappeared. Suddenly I felt nervous realizing that I was a completely different person to the one she knew, and I didn't know her now either. I lifted my hand and waited a few seconds before I knocked softly.

Chapter 12
I can't help falling...

She opened the door, and tears came to my eyes. We stared at each other for what seemed like a lifetime till it became unbearable and stepped into the room, closed the door, and held her she accepted the embrace desperately and we held each other tight, her smell, her touch. I was home. "What took you so long?" she said through tears. "I thought I lost you," I said crying. And we both held on "I will never let you go again." My mouth found its way to hers and she tasted like strawberries on a rainy day picked off the tree, it was slow and loving. She was heaven. "Where were you?" she said softly. "Lost" I smiled. "Well, you're my wife now" She nestled into my neck "I have so much to tell you" I kissed her forehead. I picked up my wife and placed her on the bed. She sat at the edge of the bed, and I got down on one knee and pulled a leather, ring box out of my back pocket. I opened the box to reveal a gold ring with a black center stone with stars. It was a ring fit for a Queen. She laughed with tears in her eyes "Oh my god, put it on, put it on!" I slipped it onto her finger and she pulled me onto the bed "I know you had your heart set on the cow's head. But I thought a galaxy was a nice touch" Lying next to her staring into her eyes "A galaxy?" I looked at her adoringly "I wanted to give you the world...the closest I got was a galaxy" She laughed into my neck as I held onto her. She jumped on top of me playfully and slowly lifting her linger slowly over her head. I wanted to savor every moment of her. I started kissing between her perfect breasts and my hand slipped from her breasts to her butt. Hanging on to her as she rubbed her clit up and down my thigh. I wanted to taste her wetness. We kissed each other lovingly our tongues exploring each other's mouths deliciously. I kissed her and grabbed her butt and put her on her back enjoying just feeling her body against mine "God, you are so beautiful" I smiled softly. She pulled me down and kissed me deeply. She was riding my thigh and moaning. It was so sexy. My hand finally made its way down to her clit. I sent slow waves of ecstasy through her body her body was shaking as she reached up for a kiss and the euphoria exploding, her pupils dilating. A connection made that was not of this world. She was moaning uncontrollably, eventually she came down from her high, while I continued to place kisses on her neck. I looked deeply into her eyes "I love you" She kissed me again softly and lovingly "I love you too" Her eyes were closed, and she fell asleep on my chest. This is heaven. She woke up and smiled at me "This is the best morning I have ever had" she said. "It is" I sighed "Waking up to my wife" She smiled and said, "Your wife, I love hearing that. Mrs Santos." I yawned.

"You do realize this is going to start War?" I held her. She looked at me "As long as you're by my side" and I looked at her seriously. "I think you should move in with me. At Willowdale" She laughed "Are you asking me to u-haul" I laughed "I'm serious, it's safe and whatever comes at us, it's the perfect safe house" She bit her lip, it was so sexy and replied with a simple "Yes." I held her and jumped. We were both laying in my bed at Willowdale, I reached over to the phone "Morning Henry, please prepare a breakfast for a Queen." And went back to holding her. "I don't have any clothes or anything" she laughed "I had Henry bring some of your stuff over and this is your card the limit is half a million but as my wife you have signing power for anything you want." She looked at me "You never gave up, did you" I smiled sadly "I thought you died but something in me wouldn't let go." I said staring into her eyes.

Eventually, we got out of bed. Enjoying the spread Henry had prepared. Enjoying amazing coffee with her and even laughing and making fun of each other even discussing Honeymoon Plans "Anywhere except Ethiopia, they kinda hate me" I laughed then my phone rang. It was Lu. I answered, "Did you by any chance kill three cows?" I replied "Yes" I feel him freaking out "Did you also threaten to drop an atomic bomb on the holy land and marry the princess?" he sounded urgent. "Also, yes" I replied.

"Well then buck up bitch because Michael and Prince Ahmed have just declared war against us because of some Israeli purity shit......"

Chapter 13
Something Wicked This Way Comes...

Now don't get me wrong. I love witches. They would always be my council before war.... Like I said, I admire the witches of all the species created. Not only did they outlive the countless eradications. They are the reason we are all here. Magic.... They were cunning, rude even complete assholes but never evil. You read that right and with any species you get good ones and bad ones...but evil. That's something else. My Dad started "Why don't you have some whisky?"

A glass was already poured and the waiter brought it next to me. I smiled and thanked him. Taking the glass politely. Subtly...very subtly a shift in energy as I slowly drew the glass to my lips, I smiled "Belladonna..." I put the glass down "Cute, I suppose...so was that your way of getting rid of me?" I sat forward. "Tell me what I need to know, and you will never have to see me again." There was an awkward pause, so I grabbed my phone," Are you at the club?" He replied something incoherent "I'm at my parents throw up a bottle" and a beautiful bottle of Whiskey appeared in my hand "This is why you're my best friend," I said to myself before I opened and drank from the bottle. I could see the questions. But I didn't care. "Given your lovely welcome, I'm going to assume you are not Hecte just a witch. And you Mr Santos. Failed to mention the human sacrifice part at the council meeting... linked by our Willowdale ancestors or rather 'The Scribes of Judas'?" This got a reaction.

My father clenched his jaw unimpressed. "How did you know?" He said almost snarling. Sitting, I put my foot on my knee (The lesbian crossing of the legs) "Well Father, if you must know after I bought the place, I wanted to remodel. I found out once I returned from that shitshow of a council..." He wanted to scream at me but instead said "How do you know?" I lit a cigarette "Well that Principal...That Principal made me an offer I couldn't refuse. "200 million dollars with the comment 'It belongs in your family'" I continued...now stop giving me the run-around. I have a pregnant, finance planning a wedding at home, so I am highly susceptible to violence" I said louder and more irritable than intended.

This made my mother's mouth fall open. "Please tell me you did not get that girl pregnant?" I laughed to myself "Mum, not only did I get her pregnant. We tired our knots. So let it go because at this point you guys barely have an invitation to the wedding". My mother looked at me. Fuming "And where did you get 200 million dollars to buy Willowdale?" I clenched my jaw. "I may not have always known what my powers were. But I was always resourceful even if you couldn't see it."

My mother started hesitantly "As you found out, our blood isn't exactly the purest, I was born of a witch that betrayed blessed be the Goddess. She did take pity on my pregnant mother, but we were stripped of our powers, only able to practice herbology, and as you already know, your father is a descendant of Judas. Had your father gone to Willowdale he would have been sacrificed as well...So we ran...To the suburbs. We honestly thought the hatred in that camp would shield you, just like whatever was dug up in these mine dumps that created a natural shield. From all magic. You can't honestly tell me you believed it was a coincidence that you grew up down the road from a princess?" She stopped but honestly, I was surprised I was getting something "So we set up a home, but we desperately wanted a child. So, we made a deal..." My mother stopped. "A deal?" I asked "With the devil..." my father jumped in "We needed to separate you. They would always be looking for you. No matter where you hid. God alone knows what they would do to you. We didn't care that you were a lesbian. The Muslims would hang you, skin you, rape you if meant protecting the Princess...and there would be nothing your father and I could do." I paused "You said you made a deal with the Devil? What did he look like?" My parents looked confused "That's your question?" I had a serious look on my face. "The Devil?" I said humorously. "As in the Christians God's Devil?" I tried to hold back laughing.

"Ok, we are going to something stronger than whiskey." I laughed I pulled out a bottle of Aquadent and poured everyone a shot "So do you want the good news or the bad news first?" My parents looked shocked. I've never seen them look shocked. "But firstly, I must say it is ridiculous that we are still paying for Juda's terrible negotiation skills."

Chapter 14

The truth will set you free, but it will piss you off first.

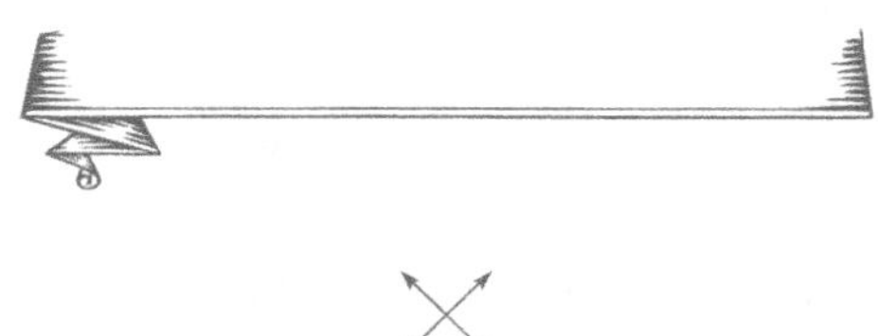

"OK LET'S START WITH the bad news." There was no point in sugarcoating any of it "Bad news, you had a natural birth...I have blood from you and Dad. I don't know who you made a deal with, but it wasn't the Devil. My blood was polluted when a siren fed off me when I was 8 but my body got rid of it because when she left, I threw it up. So, like 2% siren and then the blood deal I made with the devil, it was a mixed so more of a bind. So sorry but I am in fact by blood. "I took another drink. As they sat there with their mouths open.

I savored my drink when my phone rang "Hey beautiful, I miss you already..." I could hear the chaos behind her "Don't you 'beautiful' me, where are you I'm drowning weddings take time and I feel like I'm in a war zone. Did you know you get shades of white?" I took a quick swig "Babes this is putting a lot of pressure on the baby and you.... I asked Henry to have a plane waiting for you. I have decided that you and your bridesmaids are going to have the bachelorette party of your dreams. And when you get back. I would have pulled off the wedding of the century. One worthy of a queen. Just take your dresses and when you land. The weddings of fairytale will be waiting for you." I could hear her smile through the phone "Enjoy the holiday and I can't wait to be

91

married to the love of my life." "She started crying- hormones - "I love you so much" "Don't cry love...it will be more than you than you can dream of. We'll be safe with our beautiful family. I love you; your spa day starts now, and I am counting the days...I love you..." she paused before she put the phone down "I love you to."

"Sorry about that...where were we?........ Ouma didn't mention she mended our sins against Hecte...our coven ran...assuming that Hecte had cursed us...but Ouma didn't. Not shocking...she was badass." My mother looked at me livid and upset. I closed the doors with pulses. "No one leaves, till we figure this out." I had a straight look on my face like I was done with the bullshit "Which leaves Judas? And the 'devil you made a deal' situation. Would you care to enlighten us?" I looked at my father. "Well...we summoned the devil..." he was stuttering "And we got pregnant...." I looked at him not believing a word. "Pray tell, what did this devil look like?" I said grinding my teeth. "And who the fuck are the Scribes of Judas?"

My father rubbed his forehead. He downed his drink. "After the crucifixion, Judas and a few of his followers ran, Judas didn't leave for 30 pieces of silver...Judas loved Jesus that's why he did what was asked of him. Jesus asked Judas to betray him...and when he fled it wasn't because of the money. It was because of the secrets he was entrusted with and the forbidden love he had for Jesus. The archangel Michael also visited him. Showing him things that were forbidden to humans." I looked at my father "Michael wouldn't have happened to have passed on some scrolls, would he?" I said bluntly. My father's eyebrows shot up. "Well, that explains why he's been such a pain in my ass." My father looked distraught "Judas and his followers documented everything...which caused war to break out between Willowdale and the Vatican. We don't know how, but we started to develop abilities..." He took a sip of his drink. "But we needed peace. So, we sat down with the pope himself. We agreed to get rid of the scrolls casting them out into a void and every year sacrifice one of our offspring as penance."

I shook my head "You know...you guys suck at negotiating. What did we get?" My father looked at me "They would leave us alone, provided Judas was not mentioned at Willowdale." I laughed and looked at him "So what? Willowdale became a meat factory? Fuck, you people are unbelievable. Train us then hunt us for sport?" My father looked at me with disgust "No human should have such knowledge." The look on my face clearly showed that I gave zero fucks. "So, who did you make a deal with? And what exactly did you offer up?" My father looked at me dead in the eye "God made us in pairs...so I offered yours. You could still have a chance at normal even if you didn't marry your soulmate, and we could still have heirs even if you were alone." My jaw clenched and stood up. I buttoned my blazer pulled out an envelope and threw it on the table. "That's a wedding invitation. I want you to have a front-row seat when I marry the love of my life you son of bitch...and you, mother, are by far the worst witch I have ever met, and I've met a few." I laughed, I downed my drink you can only listen to stupid for so long. And with that, I jumped down to Lu.

A man that wasn't Henry welcomed us into the parlor "I'm sorry and your name is?" He looked nervous "My apologies Ma'am, I'm Jeffery and I will be serving you tonight." I looked him up and down "And Henry interviewed you?" I asked, "Yes Ma'am" I was hesitant to say the least "Why don't you get us a drink and give us a minute?" He quickly mixed some blue drink for Lu; it had flowers and an umbrella. "A blue lagoon for the gentlemen and a bottle of whiskey for the lady" I was impressed, Henry had sent me Jefferys's credentials. So, I didn't have to worry about snitches. "You know…" I said to Lu "You are the gayest, straight man I know." He rolled his "Taste doesn't have a gender…he'll be here in 20" He checked his phone. I scrolled my phone replying to an 'I miss you' text and replying to emails about the wedding with the co-ordinator. "You know what I don't get?" I said both of us still looking at our phones." What?" he replied, more interested in his phone. "The good guys get everything, the money, the power, the fame even the girl. You are given everything on a silver platter. Why are they losing? That shitshow they created themselves. Were we just created to be the scapegoat? Someone to fear and a hero to love?" I paused "That's fucked up." Lu finished my sentence "Another level of insecurity" still not looking up from his phone.

The room was quiet you could only hear the crackle of the fire and typing on our phones. It was calm and restful till a bright light filled the room, with the song Johnny Hallyday's L'instinct playing as Michael descended with his wings open, he was probably the most beautiful man I have ever seen but I couldn't help myself. I burst out laughing "And I thought you were the dramatic one." I told Lu through laughter. My sides started to hurt.

Chapter 15
Michael, Michael, Michael....

Seeing my laughter Michael spoke, "Clearly my presence here isn't being taken seriously, maybe should just leave." I continued to giggle "Oh, relax...just because the very elaborate gay entrance that you use to intimidate people didn't work, that doesn't mean we can't have a civilized conversation." I smiled at him, clearly holding back a giggle. "Come, sit and have a drink with us," I said casually. "I must say you are the most beautiful man I have ever seen, God truly spent time on perfection...but ran out of brain cells" Lu spat into his drink. Flattery will get you everywhere and it's not like he understands. "Thank You," he said and sat down. "No, I should say thank you...for taking time out of your busy day, to protect the people of Isreal. We just have a few questions about Judas." I said with a smile. He had a serious look on his face "I cannot reveal what I told him." He said "I didn't expect you to. I just needed confirmation that you did." He looked at me with the same face and a dead look in his eyes "And you delivered the message of course." His nostrils began to flare. 'Got you' I thought "Thank that's all we wanted to know. Relax we are all friends here...I must say I was very shocked at the whole Lut situation." He relaxed "Yes drastic measures had to be taken to ensure that the sin of homosexuality didn't spread," He said casually "I know I'm beautiful, but I can't imagine it would be instinct to rape me...no self-control I tell you." He confidently. I laughed "Yes...imagine being a woman." I kept a smile plastered on my face. "The meteor was ingenious was that your idea?" I said trying to look impressed. He laughed as Jeffery presented him with a drink. "It was actually" He smiled very proud of himself "It erased whatever sin plagued that land" He continued. I smiled "I would imagine it would erase a lot" laughing "I'm curious though, they were so taken by your beauty they wanted to rape you?" I said feigning shook "Well I guess to most I'm too gorgeous to resist." I giggled with him. Check.

"Yeah, except rape isn't about lust, rape is about power, but that's a lie you just spun stuck. That mob came at you, maybe they didn't want you. They wanted something way more powerful..." Micheal pulled back, his body clearly in defensive mode now "If I had to put money on it, I would say..." I pretended like I was thinking very hard "The Akashi Records perhaps?" I pretended like I was thinking of swirling my glass. "A meteor could destroy that...unless it just flew into the sea..." A fake worried look appeared on my face "I mean that would be highly forbidden? We are not meant to know certain things, second only to the apple and look what happened there" Again, feigning shock. The look on his face was priceless. "Now I'm going to say this very nicely. I don't know why you didn't give Judas the scrolls and frankly, I don't care. But you're going to stay out of my way as I attempt to fix this shitshow the 'Heros' have made. You are going to practice some self-control and not declare war every time you don't like something...and maybe if you spent less time on your hair, Palestine wouldn't be in the state that it is." Mate

That was the first time I saw him look scared. "You wouldn't." I stood up "The only reason you are alive is because you're Lu's brother. So, please. Test my patience." He looked down "I will stay out of the way." He said grudgingly "Good Michael. Now descended up, the same way you came down. Or dare I say, you can fight with us. That is if you have any honor at all."

Still looking down he gave me a defeated nod "Jeffery please show our guest to his room." Lu looked at me half shocked with his mouth open, half impressed "That.... was badass."

I took out my phone and messaged.

Me: there's the ever-present thin layer of radiation and particles and random particles. It will be empty, there's no meaningful structure...till now. I trust you received the gift I sent.

C: Delivered. How the hell did you pull this one off?

Me: Do you even have to ask? Astral projection.

I looked at Lu "We have 3 days." I was worried about the timeline "Jesus did it" Lu said, "Jesus is a prick as we both saw he sent the world's worst fucking break-up text in history" Lu lifted his eyebrow getting excited. "You have an idea..." he said in a tone that clearly showed his relief. "I don't have an idea.... I have a concept of an idea..."

I picked up my phone and started typing.

Me: Are we good?

C: Most of it.

Me: That's a lot.

C: Not if you feel its energy.

Me: We don't have that kind of time.

C: Your call. It would be easier just to move the whole thing.

Chapter 16
Three days till the wedding....

Already telling me it's going to be a busy day. "Good morning beautiful, I just got a call from my mother saying that she received the invitation. She seemed surprised." Salma said shocked. "Well, I did send you a copy, I know the fingerprint travel isn't ideal, but it is the safest," I said hoping she wouldn't be upset. "No... it's perfect. It's so beautiful and it makes me wonder exactly where we are getting married..." It was cute when she was trying to fish. "Hmmm still not going to tell you but I think you'll like it. How's the Bachelorette going? Anyone I need to worry about?" I laughed "You're funny." She said sarcastically. "It's amazing, I can't believe you rented us an island!" She laughed, "You call Lu the dramatic one, but everything you do is over the top." We both laughed at the "My love it's not about dramatic, it's about giving you everything you want and more." I said looking at my phone to see a text come through "I have to go but only 3 more days till we have the best sex of our lives" She laughed "You are ridiculous." She deadpanned "I love you." I said trying to be cute. "I love you too." And with that, we both put down.

The message was from Fernando Da Silva a member of the Scribes.

Fernando: Floor plan of the Vatican as requested.

Me: Nice. See you at the meeting.

I went to the war room. Judas was looking amazing, but he did need something to calm him down. So, I may have swayed his emotions somewhat. As I looked around the room, I saw Henry explaining something to the scribes, I saw Lu going through the possible allies, even Judas was trying to piece together this puzzle we were dealing with. In that moment I paused. These walls had seen enough death. We had seen enough death. Every person in this room. Fuck every bad guy had to suffer through injustice they didn't deserve purely because it would fit their narrative. In the pit of my stomach, I got that feeling. You know, that destructive 'Fuck this' feeling. I stood up "Look everyone, we will meet at 10 am tomorrow. Go home. Spend time with your loved ones" Everyone looked confused at first, but my face simply said 'trust.'

I made my way back to my chambers. Time to go to basics. I sat on the floor of our bedroom; it felt so empty without Salma. I had 3 black candles and sand from my ancestral graveyard. I took a deep breath. But first I decided to go for a walk, soaking up as much pain as possible...my eyes turned red, and my head split with a migraine, I kept going through the woods for about 2 hours, but it felt like forever. I touched as much as I could. I also made a point to gather some sand and earth.

I was finally back in my room. In front of the candles. Placing the soil with the water. Now all I had to do was focus. Not my strong point. I calmed myself and lit the candles. My head was still splitting but I focused on Chaos. "I call forth the God Chaos. As I, a daughter of Hecte, implore you to manifest for if you don't, I shall pull you from the realm against your will. Hecte allow me to correct injustice, allow them to reap what they sow!" The candles burnt brighter as I cut the palm of my hand and let it drip onto the flames. It was working. Pieces of Chaos began to fill the room. I stood up. He looked unimpressed but molecules were still making the way to him. I could feel the void fill my chest and he started becoming whole and I picked up the sand I had gathered outside. I rubbed it into my cut and continually felt and rubbed it on my hand.

He was completed and he looked pissed. "Sorry about the entrance, but I heard we're family!" I said with a falseness. "I've been looking for you." He said through gritted teeth. "And I have been waiting for you...I'm surprised it took you so long." I smiled "What did I do to you again?" I said stumped. This seemed to piss him off even more. "I came to collect. I hear I got a two-for-one special" he laughed manically. I smiled at him with disgust "Oh darling, you're about to get much more than two." I laughed at myself. That wasn't the right thing to do because he pushed me through the wall using part of a void. I stood up in the dust and rubble "Did I say something?" Needless to say, I went flying again. This time out the window. I stood up and smiled "Big mistake...I am a daughter of Hecte and a descendent of Judas...I feel the power from the void that you are..." He pushed me again this time I think I did a 360. I was bleeding I must have cut my lip. "Except there is something in your void isn't there? It is vast but you did create something" Another push. Ok so he wasn't much of a talker, but he was an ass "I will die before I let you near my family." I went down on one knee and placed my hand in the dirt "Now you will reap what you sow." I could feel the energy passing through me and blasting Chaos. "A void filled with hate is no longer a void. All the Chaos you've caused, the hate, the pain. It's about time We give some of it back." My body was throbbing with pain, but I refused to stop until there was no space for him to harness energy. "Now you get to live with the Chaos you've caused." He fell to his knees, blood coming out of his eyes, ears, and nose yet he still mustered up enough to say "It will still be Chaos. Even if I'm powerless." That statement pissed me off even more causing more energy to flow through "You don't know who I am." I said standing up. He was on the floor, coughing up blood "You can't kill a God with a mortal weapon" I lifted my sword. Thank you, Mother Superior. I thrust the sword into his heart and pushed Every emotion, every moment of self-loathing all that pain and hardship eliminated by 5 little words. "I claim who I am" I screamed because none of this was coincidental. Every moment worked in unison to lead to this. It was fate. Not Chaos. He turned to ash. I put my sword away in my trusty pouch when suddenly a statue of him appeared. He looked like a Greek God that was sculptured to perfection. I stood there. "Pain in the ass," I mumbled to myself as I walked back inside. Henry and Lu came running probably because of the ruckus. "Sorry Henry," I said casually but still out of breath "But we needed that statue." Henry and Lu looked flabbergasted as I limped back to my room.

Chapter 17
Two days till the wedding....

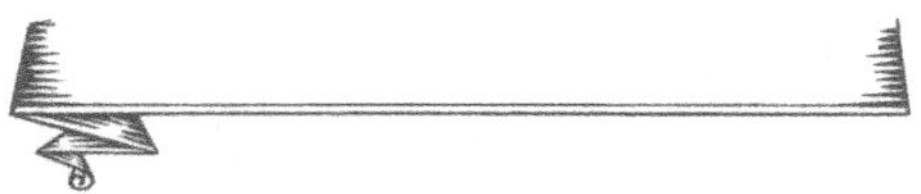

We sat for breakfast the next day, but you could cut the tension with a knife. Eventually, Lu cracked "So are we going to talk about the fact that you killed a God yesterday?" Lu said rolling his eyes at the fact that he needed to ask. He was annoyed at me, but as much as I wanted to address that we got an unexpected visitor. The double doors suddenly opened. I wiped my mouth and stood up quickly. "Mother Superior" My eye went big, but I bowed "Francesca, may we have the room." I looked at Henry and Lu and they could see the fear in my eyes, so they politely excused themselves. "Please sit." I pulled out a chair "Can I get you anything?" Mother Superior was not playing "No thank you, as much as I love your banter I'm going to get straight to the point. The Vatican is not yours to take." She said sternly. I sat down and I think my mouth opened but nothing came out. "The Nuns deserve to be in charge. They had no issue kicking us out after the wars and the sacrifices we have made. The nuns will be taking back the Vatican" I was surprised to hear this but like I told you before Nuns are badass. There was no question in my mind what my answer would be. I smiled and calmly said "I couldn't agree more. We will stand with you against the Vatican. Our intention was never to take power. Just to stop the injustice of the leaders. So, Sister how can I be of assistance" I lifted a wine glass, and she lifted hers and we both smiled. "You now have the full backing of hell, The scribes of Judas, and an army of sirens behind you. As they only revealed 135 men which I don't believe for a second. So, whatever the plan, consider us in."

We moved to the war room. Muhammed, another descendent of Judas had the floor plan of the Vatican up and was explaining "Every catholic country would be willing to send troops. If we go in guns blazing, we may start a war that never stops. It could go on for years maybe centuries." He continued "Vatican City is brainwashed. They won't take this lying down. However, our allies have gathered intel that the council and the pope will meet today at sunset" We sat listening. I finally spoke "Muhammed I'm sorry I never took the time to get to know you...or anyone at Willowdale...This is truly amazing what you came up with here." I finished "Yes Thank you, Muhammed" Mother Superior added. "This presents us with the perfect opportunity. They are all going to be in the same place at once. We can kill every last one of them and still be home in time for supper." My eyebrow raised involuntarily. This is why I loved her. "Sister if I may?" She looked at me with an expression I couldn't read. "Yes, you may." She said with a straight face. "I, more than anyone, enjoy a good old-fashioned bloodbath and honestly, I would say that we hang them in the time square but what if I could make that they voted you a leader? As Muhammed said the catholic countries are brainwashed. They need to hear from the Pope himself that he's putting you in charge. As for the council...we do what generations before us have done" Mother Superior looked at me "And what have they done." I had a naughty grin "Lead by fear and slowly you can vote each one of them out. Without the rest of the world knowing. Can anyone here actually name a council member?" I looked around the room "I undressed them and covered them in blood, and I can't remember one name." Fernando looked at me strangely "What?" Mother Superior cut in "And if this doesn't work?" I looked Mother Superior dead in the eye "Then we do it your way. Take it by force." Mother Superior thought for a moment and finally "Ok and how long will it take to infiltrate the Vatican?" She asked. I looked at her "Maybe a few seconds?" Mother Superior looked at me, her face clearly saying 'There is no way in hell this works' but finally replied "Very well, we leave at sunset" Judas stood up and "There is a chance that your powers may be rendered useless as it is consecrated land. Your blood has to be pure..." This surprised me but I replied with "What does pure mean? I mean isn't it run by the mafia?" Judas looked at me "What is a mafia?"

"I don't think Mother Superior should accompany us. If we don't have powers. We may have to shed blood." Mother Superior gave me a look "I can't promise that we won't fight. We weren't relying on backup." I thought for a second "I can respect that but is it possible to buy us 2 hours? Then we will fully support the invasion." Mother Superior looked sternly at me "2 hours. Not a minute longer."

Lu looked at me "Don't you think for a second, I'm not coming with you. You already killed one God without me, and I am not missing the action." I looked at him "I don't understand how the church hates homosexuals when every angel I've met is soooooo gay." I said with a face.

Chapter 18
Mama said there'll be days like this...

Sunset came swiftly. Lu and I were ready. Wearing our swords on our belts. And so, we jumped into the Circus of Nero, The Vatican Obelisk in St Peters Square. Hoping there may be tourists giving us the element of surprise. I was wrong. We had jumped directly into an ambush of guards with guns...and Judas was right. We couldn't use our powers but I thought fast and threw Lu. I stood in the middle circled by guards, sword out. When a woman appeared.

"Mother..." I put my sword down, now I was just irritated. "I would say I'm surprised..." My mother smirked at me "Still think I'm the worst witch you know? Did you think that would be our last conversation" I laughed "Since when did the church work with witches?" She let out a sinister laugh. "Oh, my child. We are basically all pagans...in the end at least." The council appeared behind her. My hands were bound, and I was brought to my knees with a hit of a musket on the back of my kneecaps. Taking my sword and hitting me in the face with the pommel. They looked pissed. I laughed "What color is YOUR Bugatti?" I need to learn to shut my mouth. "Put her in the stocks. Now" One of them said. The guards dragged me off. Here we go again. If it was just a pole, I would already know what to do but this. This was going to be tricky but on the upside it would probably only last two hours. But as fate would have it. Five minutes later.

Back-to-back, swords up, shields ready. There are many definitions of love but for me, it was rather simple. Love the woman that you would go to war for but marry the woman that wouldn't let you go alone. And what can I say we were in the middle of a shit storm. "You didn't think I'd leave you to your own devices, did you?" Within seconds Salma had wielded her sword with enough force to lock and break its hinges off the pillory then immediately turned back to face the soldiers circling, her stance strong,

She threw me a sword and I grabbed the grip. I saw white light much like a vision or memory, a flash of hope. Babies floating on clouds. I remembered this except this time, it wasn't a woman at the gates. It was a little girl and she said "Soon Mama" and she smiled. It was a split second, and I was back fighting next to the love of my life. With sword in hand, I made my way to Salma with vigor. With her back against mine "My partner in crime" I smirked "Shall we kill these ornaments or are we feeling merciful?" As I finished the sentence Salma was blowing white dust over the soldiers. As the soldiers inhaled, their eyes turned black. Salma stood like the warrior and screamed "Corpus tuum et mens mea nunc sunt! You have just inhaled a highly concentrated dose of MD- The malleable death." The soldiers had blood slowly dripping out of their eyes, most falling to the ground in agony. "What you are feeling now is the poison engraining itself in your cell wall. Obey me and live and you will die an agonizing death. You belong to me now!" I stood behind her in attack mode but her taking charge like this was so.... sexy. "Assemble, guns down, and do not move" Almost immediately every soldier moved, almost robot-like created a typical legion formation. Salma moved with intent like she knew exactly where she was going, I grabbed her, and I followed her lead. "How did you know where I was?" making sure I was aware of our surroundings. "You sent Lu back...he told us." I had a confused look on my face. "I pushed Lu out of the danger...." Salma even though we were on high alert, didn't have to see me to know that I was confused "You didn't push him. You threw him back"

Still following her "My powers work. How?" I asked her. "Stop." I pulled Salma back "The camaras start here" I pushed us between two columns. With just enough space for our bodies to be pressed together. I could feel her breath on my neck as snuggled into it "You know I have had a fantasy about fucking in the pulpit" I smirked. Salma just giggled into my chest. "We have 1 hour and 30 minutes to stop war. We need to focus she said kissing me. "That we do..." I continued. "So hurry up and kill the cameras!" She said in a hushed tone. "Right..." I composed myself. I must admit. The Vatican was majestic, and we got to add these new experiences to our shared narrative. I wasn't the girl tied to the pole, left to die and I wasn't alone anymore.

I let out a pulse which killed all mechanical devices. We strolled into that meeting. It looked like a corporate conference room. Filled with the 11 descendants, the Pope himself, and my mother. "I must say, we simply wanted to request an audience but this was way more exciting," I said seriously. I could see everyone tense up. "Hello boys" I smirked "I hardly recognized you with clothes on.". The Pope stood up "What is the meaning of this? We are men of God!" He raised his voice which caused me to raise my eyebrows "No." I said completely absolute. "No?" He sneered. "You are men that I should have killed when I had the chance." I declared. "So now it's going to be so much worse." Usually it takes me much longer to focus enough to plant memories but this felt natural. They began to cry out in pain. I could imagine the headache they would have when someone was rearranging what little brains they did have. The power was pulsing out from my hand as I stared my Mother dead in the eyes. "What exactly did I do to you Mother?" I asked genuinely. Making sure Salma was behind me. "All I ever wanted was your approval..." I said, sadness dripping from my words. Her cold exterior slowly melting. "You're an abomination." She said as if it was undeniable. I stopped the pulses. Their heads hit the table. It was done. "I could kill you..." I started calmly "But death is too good for you." I put out my hand for Salma to hold so that we could leave. "Oh, and one more thing, if you do anything to disrupt this wedding, I will put you in a box and throw it in the ocean," I said casually.

Salma and I walked out, I pulled her closer and kissed her temple. "I love you," I said. She gave me a sad smile "I'm sorry..." she started. "...what she said...it was so cruel." She finished with tears in her eyes. I turned to face her and held her cheeks with both my hands putting my forehead on hers and with a soft smile I said "Don't cry, my love...I am standing under the Sistine Chapel with the world's most beautiful woman, who also happens to be the mother of my child. And that is the most miraculous thing ever and so worth everything I had to do to get here. If that means I'm an abomination, then I will gladly scream it from the rooftops!" we giggled with happy tears in our eyes.

Ten minutes later Mother Superior appeared with her advisors. They found us in the Sistine Chapel. "As promised sister. The minute they wake up they will elect you as their leader." I said. Salma took out the MD powder and politely handed it to Mother Superior "And from now on the army will only take their orders from you." Salma added with a smile. "Congratulations Sister. I can't think of anyone more deserving..." I paused "and in light of our gentlewomen's agreement and peace at last I present a gift, given in good faith. The Arc of the Covenant."

Mother Superior looked at me dumbfounded and after a silent pause filled with awe, she just hugged me with tears in her eyes. "Sister, I know it's against the church but we're getting married tomorrow. It would be an honor if you could be there...Of course, we understand if it goes against your values..." Mother Superior looked at me offended "Why would you ask me that?" I was caught off guard. "Don't be preposterous! I am the Mother of the brides... I need to be there to assist." Salma and I giggled with relief. I didn't say anything even though the tears had already started to flow and I just pulled Mother Superior in for a long, tight hug. "We have to get to the wedding venue; I'm already breaking enough rules. We shouldn't see each other the night before the wedding. It's bad luck" We laughed but Salma took my hands "See you soon Sister" I smiled as we jumped.

Chapter 19
The night before.

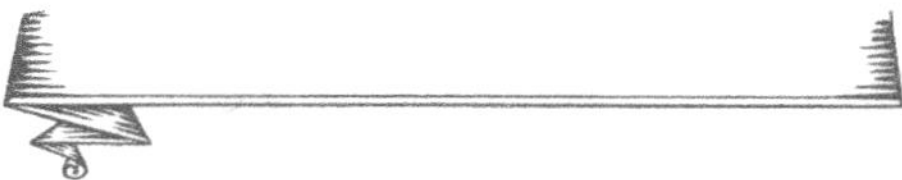

We landed in the most beautiful garden, with flowers I'm not even sure had been discovered yet. It was purely majestic. "Where are we?" Salma asked. I smiled and said "This is The Library of Alexandria, a sanctuary of learning, and a symbol of human aspiration, it ignited a flame of inquiry that knew no bounds. It unites us across cultures and eras, illuminating the path toward discovery, wisdom, and hope...it's also our wedding venue" I was holding her. I kissed her slowly savoring every second, every exquisite taste because there was finally peace. "Oh my God!" she pulled away "Are you serious? How did you..." She was cut off by Charlotte, who came running. She jumped into my arms "Charlotte!" I said excitedly. "You look amazing!" she did "And look at you! Turning grey..." she noted matching my excitement. Her eyes went big trying to hint "Charlotte this is Salma" I said.

Charlotte wasted no time and immediately went in for a hug "I've heard so much about you...and don't worry about tomorrow I have rooms for you and your bridesmaids for tonight and to get ready for tomorrow" She said beaming "Oh my God, I've heard so much you!" Salma added. They were holding each other's hands and jumping with excitement "Tomorrow is going to be amazing!" Charlotte said eagerly "And you! Off to the bachelor pad, you cannot see the bride the night before the wedding and Lu is on the way." She hushed me away. "Ok, ok...I'm going" I raised my hands and left to the bachelor pad which looked a lot like the gentlemen's club.

Architecturally, the Library was a marvel, designed to accommodate scholars and thinkers from diverse backgrounds. Its vast halls, adorned with intricately carved columns and illuminated by sunlight filtering through large windows, exuded an atmosphere of tranquillity and reverence—shelves lined with scrolls—some exquisitely decorated—held the collective wisdom of civilizations. The ambiance was steeped in history, with towering shelves lined with scrolls and books that whispered tales of love and knowledge from centuries past. Decorated with delicate flowers and twinkling fairy lights, the library transformed into an ethereal haven, a perfect blend of the old and the new.

The next day came swiftly but Charlotte made the reception venue a magnificent dream. The color scheme was light pastel shades, resembling pale blue-grey or white stone., ornate cathedral-like structure. The architecture is highly detailed, with pointed arches, tall columns, and intricate carvings. Vines and greenery have climbed over and are growing profusely along the walls and towers of the building. Various sizes of trees and bushes are planted in a formal garden layout surrounding the structure. The garden beds and walkways are paved with light gray stone. Stone balustrades and stairways are visible, leading up to and around the building. The background includes a dense backdrop of forest trees, creating a dramatic contrast between the structure and the natural setting. The light suggests a sunny day, casting shadows near the building.

Lu and I got ready in the bachelor suite. Lu had a bright red suit on, which he was very proud of. I stuck with the traditional suit that mirrored the dignified grace of the ancient philosophers. Lu fixed my tie. "Are you sure?" he asked seriously. I smiled. "I've been dreaming of her since I was a child. I was born to be hers...so yes, I'm ready"

There were tears, smiles, and cheering all around. Mother Superior grabbed me before I took my place at the altar. She pulled me in for a hug with tears and in her eyes she whispered "I'm so proud of you." Henry walked her down the aisle, and all I could do was thank God...because we made it.

As the ceremony commenced, the air was filled with Canon in D, a sweet melody played by a small ensemble, crafting the soundtrack. Francesca's heart swelled with joy knowing that echoes promise of love, in that sacred space, under the watchful eyes of history, Frankie, in a crisp suit that mirrored the dignified grace of the ancient philosophers standing nervously at the end of the aisle with Lu and Charlotte that agreed to be the officiant. La Via en rose began to play, everybody stood up as Fathima looked radiant in her flowing gown, adorned with intricate lace reminiscent of the scrolls surrounding them. Then finally...

As the soft strains of La Via en Rose filled the air, all eyes turned to the entrance of the aisle, where a beautiful bride made her grand entrance. She glided gracefully, her gown flowing like a gentle wave, the delicate lace and satin catching the light with every step. The dress, intricately designed, hugs her figure perfectly before cascading into a stunning train that trails behind her, adding an ethereal quality to her presence. I held back my tears and asked myself what I did to deserve so much love.

As she approached the altar, everyone was captivated by her grace and elegance, and a sense of love and anticipation filled the space. We stood, holding each other hands and finally, I heard the words I wanted to for so many years Charlotte started "Ladies and gentlemen, we are gathered here today to witness the commitment of love between two of the strongest women I have ever had the honor of meeting. And so, woven through the pages of their book of life, Francesca and Salama will fill every chapter with love, adventure, learning, and the unwavering promise to support and uplift one another." Charlotte paused "The couple have decided to write their vows. Salma, would you like to start?"

Salma started with tears in her eyes "I have prepared a poem that I wrote when I thought I had lost:

You consume every thought in my head
While capturing every fiber of my being
I try to resist
But I'm powerless against your gaze
Like a moth to a flame
I am powerless
But even if I could resist your fiery beauty
I wouldn't.

So I wait...
For the will of Allah
A plan much greater than mine
So I wait...
All the while...
I remain
Only yours.

There wasn't a dry eye in the room. I looked deeply into her eyes. Happy tears in our eyes. Charlotte spoke again "Frankie?" I started "A much smarter, wiser person than me said "Life seeks out the light" and before I met you, all I knew was darkness. So I danced with the shadows, thinking 'Well at least I'm drunk' Soft laughter came from the crowd. "I'm glad I was though otherwise; I wouldn't have found you. It was dim at first, far off into the distance. And the closer I got to feeling something I hadn't felt since I was a child...It was hope. Hope is a funny emotion because it's good, yet terrifying. You terrified me." More laughter and smiles "but I knew I would never leave this light because it gave me life again... Like the sun to the earth. So I sat and thought how I could ever repay you. At first, I thought to promise that you would always have my sword, I would protect you, no matter what the consequences, and then we went into battle, time and time again and I realized you were always the one that saved me and for the first time I didn't feel alone in this battlefield we called life... You didn't run.." I was choking up. "Then I thought I could offer you my heart but that seemed too easy because it already belonged to you. So I decided to give you my stars, my light as you so willingly gave me yours. My love will persist till the last star in the sky burns out. Many will condemn our love but if hell is our fate then we shall take over and I can think of no one better reason for battle. Plus everyone knows you just came for the food" Lu and I gave each other a look and everyone laughed. "You may now kiss the bride" and everybody cheered as I held Salma in my arms and kissed her passionately. Finally...

Lu and I made our way to the Bachelor pads we couldn't see much I suppose Charlotte didn't want the surprise to be as effective as possible. And we were not disappointed. We approached as we opened the door we were met with the abundant greenery interwoven throughout the structure, climbing the columns and walls, creating a lush, almost overgrown effect. The greenery is various shades of deep and lighter greens. The high ceiling features a decorative, stained-glass-like pattern in shades of blue and gold. Steps lead down the center of the image towards a focal point. The floor appears to be a polished, light-gray stone or marble with a decorative pattern of emerald-green tiles/mosaics—a full interior shot of a whimsical, multi-story library. The library features a spiraling staircase that winds around multiple levels, each containing bookshelves filled with books. I looked at Lu "We should just get some rest." I spoke. Lu gave me a look.

"What? I say?" Lu's mouth flew open in a dramatic. "You didn't have a bachelor party! But don't stress, your best friend Lu took the liberty of having enough mead delivered to last us a week and the guys are coming!" he said excitedly. This made me turn my head "Who are the guys?" He started assembling the most advanced gin and tonic bar with garnishes sided with Cuban cigars. I had to admit it was the best gentlemen's spread ever. He then next the Cuban cigars. He brought out a cheese board with relishes, some I didn't even recognize. He then proceeded to pair the wine with the cheese...and then he polished it off with a topless mixologist. My mouth was open. "You've done this before?" I asked. Lu looked at me "No I haven't..." he said, thinking "No one has ever asked me to be their best man before. My face softened. I grabbed him and held him tight. "I have never had a best friend. No one has thrown a party. What did I do to deserve you?" We were both laughing Happy Tears. The bachelor pad itself was a marvel the walls and architectural details of the library are dark, ornate, and Gothic-inspired. Extensive greenery is visible through large windows that frame the lush forest outside. Plants and vines cascade down the exterior walls and inside the library. Dark, rich-colored furnishings, including a velvet teal-colored sofa and low stool, are strategically placed. There was a patterned rug to give the area a homey look with similar emerald hues covering the floor. A large, ornate chandelier hanging from the ceiling and the fire created a relaxed environment.

Our moment was interrupted by a knock on the door. Lu quickly moved to the door to welcome our guests "Henry!" Lu lifted his hands to hug him "Mr. and Mrs. Dos Santos, please take a seat, a waiter will be with you shortly." He said charmingly "King Abdullah and Queen Rania Al-Yassin. Please come in, he sat them next to my parents, Jefferey he will take care of your every demand. With a smile, he helped Moher Superior to her seat at the family table. Judas finally arrived. Lu spoke to Judas seating him between Fathima and Charlotte. I could hear whispers asking where we were and how amazing the setup was. Filling their plates with finger foods and enjoying the drinks,

According to Lu, we were right on time. I was sitting when I suddenly when Salma suddenly running down. Like something out of a love story. Our favorite song playing in the background. "Kiss Me" By Sixpence Non The Richer. So I got up beaming with joy and started running towards her. Suddenly there was a tremble that lasted a few seconds. It was the tremor that marked something in the universe was mending something. "What happened to tradition?" I pulled her closed. Her cheeks were red. "I figured we were breaking all the rules anyway" She pulled me into a deep passionate kiss in front of everyone. Which may not seem out of the ordinary, but it was the first time we kissed in front of everyone. But it felt like the first time. It was unapologetic and the reason that I will always choose her.

We were interrupted by Lu "Ladies and gentlemen, I cannot thank you enough for attending Franki and Salma's bachelor party. Don't worry the stripper will be here shortly." Lu said way too seriously. I could instantly see the petrified looks on everyone's faces. "That was a joke," Lu said very seriously. Through the awkward silence. "This evening will be more about getting to know each other." I put my hand on Lu's shoulder" I smiled "If I may?" I asked "Sure…" he looked relieved " For those of you that don't know us, I am Frankie Dos Santos and this beautiful lady on my arm is Princess Salma of Jordan, and those of you that are sitting around the room that received a security clearance wedding invitation implies that you are either nearest or dearest. This event is meant to bring us together. But I do not doubt that tensions will be high." I paused but the crowd was silent. I put my hand on Lu's shoulder again " This is Lucifer Morning Star, my best man and our facilitator for the evening. You have him to thank for the amazing spread. I would like to also introduce our Officiant and wedding planner Charlotte…without her. I would not be standing here today; I looked at her thankfully., 'I gave her a knowing smile…Please feel free to indulge. Our sharing circle will start in 10 min, where Lu, my best man will take over. Thank You."

"Are we ready??" Lu yelled trying to get everyone excited. Everyone moved to the centre of the room chatting as they moved. Finally, we were ready to start. Lu started very fabulously coming in an outfit that made the rest of us feel underdressed but I couldn't help but yell "Yasss Queen" This got a few looks, But I didn't mind. You knew where the door was, flamboyantly Lu started "Now nobody panic because our first game is straight out of Grade 6" his voice showing off his crescendo. Ladies and gentlemen we shall be playing Truth and Drink!" Circling the room, filling glasses to the rim. Don't worry" he gave a sly smile we have more than enough drinks.

Finally, we were all around in a circle with our drinks in front of us and an empty wine bottle in the center. As the game maker I will spin first, those of you who have never played will be helped as we go along because it's an easy game to pick up. Salma was sitting in between my legs as I kissed her shoulder softly. Salma looked, at me as if I was crazy for being so happy. "What? It's a wedding, there's always drama?" as she giggled into my neck." Lu started the game by twisting the bottles and like fate, it landed on me. Lu let out a little chuckle and I laughed "Go easy on me. It's the first one." I said smiling. He grinned "When did you know that Salma was your hell yes. Like there's no one else. It's her and only her?" I smiled "Well from the first moment we made eye contact. I knew but when she came at me with a sword, 'I was like yip, she's the one." Everyone started laughing Judas asked, "Why did she come at you with a sword?" I giggled and replied because she thought that there was someone else...there wasn't of course." I laughed and kissed her. "My turn..." I spun the bottle and it landed on my mother " Mother. Truth or drink?" I asked. My mother sneered at me "Drink." She said dismissively and took a sip "Alright spin the bottle." She did and it landed on Mother Superior, all of us gave a cheer "Alright" my mother started "Truth or drink?" Mother Superior smiled slyly " Truth." I could see she wasn't afraid "How can you condone this abomination?" Mother Superior looked like she wanted to laugh "First of all, NO one. I mean. No one speaks about my daughters in that manner. Secondly, I would explain but that would be pointless, Because if you cannot understand how a mother can love unconditionally. Then you will never understand. I pity you. You cannot see what a brave, pure of heart, kind woman she's become, despite you two." My mother continued how could she use powers at the Vatican, dirty blood is immobilized?" The room went quiet and Mother Superior smiled "Your information was bad, clearly..." She gave a look that would sting. "Tainted blood is not the same as a pure heart. That applies to Judas down to Frankie." She spun the bottle and it landed on the Queen 'Oh fuck,' I thought.' "Truth or drink?" She paused and said "Truth" I think Mother Superior was hoping for that answer. "Your majesty, did you think that by hiding your daughter and forcing religion down her throat you could change the will of God?" The Queen's nostrils began to flare. "Nothing is impossible with Allah at your side" It was very clearly a statement. "And yet here we all sit, the night before the wedding" Mother Superior looked her dead in the eye. This was about the time Lu jumped in "Alright your turn to spin." The Queen spun the bottle and it landed on me. Great. The queen wasted no time. "What game are you playing inviting, Judas himself?" I sighed but it wasn't a sigh of defeat but rather one of a sigh that knew I wouldn't be able to explain this to stupid. "Well for starters, he is family. Secondly, questions came up about his guilt. He is a Middle Eastern man who is a slave to the words of educated white men. Men, who not only lacked morals but also men who wanted to build their fortune on the backs of those who were different. The Vatican was built by men with money but as most of these stories go, they needed scapegoats: Judas as a get-out-of-jail-free card for any sin they may commit. After all, it was his betrayal that allowed Jesus to die for everyone's sins and then of course the original scapegoat: Lucifer because after all why would we sin if it was not for Lucifer tempting us? You don't know me very well. But I hate bullies. And up until now, the Vatican has been nothing but a big bully and honestly, how can I take the Quran seriously when people are preaching hate about LGBTQIA+ rights when babies are dying in hospitals because of the Palestine and Israelis conflict? To me, it sounds like you are all a bunch of bullies hiding behind text you haven't read and I strongly suggest you all sit down and take a good long look at your priorities because consenting adults loving each other is not the same as genocide." I could see her mouth wanting to fall open, but I guess her training simply caused her to plump her lips. "How do you know this isn't a plot to escape from hell" she said softer this time like she was. " I am surprised, I expected you to ask me why I'm worthy of your daughter," I said pointedly. Her lip curled "Why do you think you're enough for her? " I sighed "I'm Franki Fucking Dos Santos and I always take receipts." I didn't even bother entertaining anything more, I just spun the bottle. Yay, it landed on my mother she chose the truth. I wanted to laugh because it was each equal parts sadness and irony. "Still trying to kill me, mother? Or did you simply come to judge?" Her eyes were dead, but I was completely apathetic "That's the wrong question." I raised my eyebrow "So what is the right question?" I asked, "The right question is if I even approve of this pseudo-wedding?" I pondered "No that's not the right question...The right question would have been if you ever actually wanted to be a mother or if this was simply about having an heir. But that one seemed kinda pointless" She looked at me somewhat surprised "Because I mean, we already know why." I said with no malice in my voice. Every around the room seemed to be at the edge of their seats. "You had the power to stop me from dying twice and for you, it was just another day. That tells me that you don't know how to be a mother and I can't blame you for that and telling me Salma was dead, showed just how calculated you were. " We stared at each other. Neither willing to stand down, I rolled the bottle over to her. Your turn." She spun the bottle and it landed on Lu. "Lucifer...did Frankie sell her soul to you?" Lu let out a laugh. "It became very clear from our meeting that I was the one selling my soul to her." He carried on laughing. "But straight answer. NO. I had to kick her out." That statement surprised everyone in the room, I assumed that was because they thought my powers came from Satan himself. 'Surprise bitches.' I laughed to myself.

Lu spun the bottle, and it slowly stopped on Charlotte. "Yass, finally," Lu said with excitement. "Ok, this question has two parts. Number one how do you know Frankie? Number 2 how did you pull this off?" he asked. Charlotte laughed at his excitement. Charlotte folded her legs "Well Frankie and I met at a conversion camp. We were 'boyfriend and girlfriend' which meant we had to share a room, God, Frankie was terrified because her abilities chose that moment to manifest." I looked at her with a sad smile "I never did thank you for that." I said softly. "Anyway, you know how hard-headed Frankie was when she was young, they tried to make her iron, so she grabbed the iron and nearly melted the Kock's face off." We both laughed at the inside joke. "Which naturally meant she got the pole." Fathima interrupted this time "The pole?" she asked. "Oh yeah, it's the pole in the sun that they tie you to without any food or water. Till they think you feel remorse...or die. Frankie was out there for 3 days, she looked like she was on her deathbed" I chimed in this time. "Which I was..." Charlotte gave a sad smile "I was standing in line for mechanics, and I saw...They wanted to make a show of her death, to show us who's in charge." She paused pondering. "I couldn't take it anymore...so I ran without thinking with the hope that I could untie her. That's when I felt the bullet go through my neck" She was lost in thought now holding the back of her neck. "She died in my arms..." my words dripping with melancholy. "And then I saw through purgatory. The kindest thing anybody has ever done for me..." I stopped her in a sad voice "You deserved so much more..." The group clearly released we were having a moment and comfortable silence fell over the group. "As for all of this, it is a small Thank you for making me the keeper of the library and bringing me back to a place that accepts me, which I think was shortly after your little excursion with Lu?" Charlotte grabbed Salma's hands "I really hope it is everything you guys deserve" she finished. I raised my glass and everyone followed "To what we all deserve. Cheers" everyone echoed "Cheers". Lu cleared his throat. "Now that we have all bonded, any more questions or can we enjoy an evening of pleasantries?" Salma's parents immediately jumped at that chance. But it was Salma who spoke first "This one is for Frankie...Why didn't you move on if you thought I was dead?" I laughed but she was serious. "Well for one. You were haunting me. It was a dim, distant light. But it was a light. And even if it was a 0.0000000001 percent chance it was you. I was willing to take it because you have also been my light, my warmth" We both had tears in our eyes as she gave me a soft short kiss...well to be fair all her kisses were too short. Our parents were livid. "I would like to emphasize again that the four of us don't agree with this!" My father yelled. His face clearly showing that they had lost control of us and the situation. "And I would like to emphasize that if you do again thing to disrupt this wedding. I will put the four of you in a box and throw you in the ocean. Are we clear?" Our parents looked shocked but this time it was the King who replied, "You're lying." He thought he could call my buff. "Oh that wasn't a threat. That was a promise." I smiled. "I wouldn't think twice." Lu looked at them trying to hold back laughter "She really wouldn't."

20 Chapter

Us...

The reception was beautiful and intimate. I was surprised when Henry came to hug me and asked if he could give a speech. I looked at him and said do you even have to ask. So before the first course was served, Henry tapped his glass with a knife to get everyone's attention. "Good Evening everyone, I know everyone is eager for the first course but I would like to say a few words. I have had the honor of raising Francesca since she was a baby. I've had the privilege of watching her grow from a rebellious teenager to this amazing politician and warrior. The last few years have been rocky as I'm sure everyone knows but whenever I brought it to her attention I was always met with 'Don't worry, I'll handle it.' Her strength silenced the neighsayers. That's not to say that she didn't do it with flair. But somehow. In some way, she always managed to ensure that justice was served. And based on that fact alone I know your grandfather would have been proud and I am proud that through all the hardships you still managed to create so many beautiful things. Salma and Frankie, you did more than just correct past injustices. You broke the stick, and you found your person against all odds and I have never seen a couple that fought so relentlessly for each other, that alone is worth celebrating." He raised his glass. To Salma and Frankie" His words echoed through the hall as I got up to give him a tight hug. He sat down. I stayed standing "I know we all hate speeches so I will be quick. First I would like to say Thank you to Salma for agreeing to marry me, to Charlotte for putting together the world's most amazing wedding, to Henry for being my rock and who should be James Bond at this point, Mother Superior-I think people underestimate how much it means to have a mother, your guidance has been invaluable, to Fathima that did judge and showed up anyway . And for Lu, my best friend, the kind that didn't ask questions but always showed up no matter how hard things were. You guys are our chosen family...and you've shown up in ways that we couldn't possibly thank you for." Salma stood up next to me "So we were going to wait but since the people we love the most surround us now in what is probably the most beautiful realm, it seems apt." We looked at each other and grinned "We're pregnant!" The entire room erupted with clapping, cheering, and whistling." The atmosphere was beautiful and supportive. This was our family.

Lu stood up "Frankie said to me once that people like us don't get happy endings, we are destined to be defeated, and to that, I can only say. You did it, bro..." He had tears in his eyes "You did it. You got the girl." He smiled at us "You know the devil doesn't exactly have people lining up to be friends" Lu was choking up but kept it together "unless they want something...but instead of making a deal... Frankie, you gave me things I never thought I would have. Love, empathy, family...you have given me so much...so given the fact that I am about to become an Uncle I felt it necessary to get my sister a rather large gift." He lifted his hands to the ceiling, and we all looked up. We were all speechless.

The Northern Lights lit up the room, displaying a natural light display. The phenomenon that occurs when charged particles from the sun collide with atoms in the Earth's atmosphere, resulting in bursts of light. There were so many colors...shades of pink, red, yellow, blue, violet and green. The lights made arcs, spirals, and curtains that danced across the room. It was mesmerizing magical and awe-inspiring. I didn't know what to say so I just pulled Lu in for a tight hug. We were both crying. Everyone was emotional as we watched the beauty. We saw a flash that looked like a shooting star. It flew landing directly on our table. The flash was startling till we realized the flash was a woman, that was dressed like Knight. She got off the table, standing firm as she took out her sword putting both hands in the grip, and kneeled before us. "Is this part of the gift?" I whispered to Lu, Lu looked highly confused "Uh No..." I shook my head awkwardly. "Thought not..."

She stood up again her sword staying in the same position. "Forgive me for disrupting your festivities but I desperately need to seek counsel with Francesca Dos Santos. She is our only hope." I looked over at Salma "I told you... it's not a wedding unless there's drama"

About the Author

A passionate educator believes in hope, love and acceptance. I live in an infinite universe in fully embracing the diversity that this world has to offer. I write to try and understand my brain which I consider alien. While many see mental illness as a downfall, I choose to embrace the emotions that I cannot control. My thoughts, my love and my and every extreme emotion that I have tried to interpret as intensely and as graphically as possible. Queer, existing my imaginary world, hopefully easing someone's pain. My book unapologetically addresses several issues with regards to religion and memorable events. Questioning the bible and the Quran. With a main character that is complicated to say the least as she disregards rules of society and religion. References to Dante's Inferno. She acts with greed as she doesn't believe good exists anymore. Packed with action as she prizes herself on her fighting and war abilities.

About the Publisher

Profile of Gabriella Da Costa

With six years of dedicated teaching experience, I have cultivated a passion for fostering a holistic and collaborative learning environment. My diverse background includes working in various educational settings, from mainstream schools to smaller boutique institutions that prioritize individualized attention and cater to the unique needs of each learner.

I am committed to encouraging a culture of positivity and friendship within the classroom, as I believe that positive social interactions are crucial for student development. By promoting an atmosphere where students feel safe and supported, I aim to enhance their overall learning experience.

Exploration is a cornerstone of my teaching philosophy. I emphasize the importance of learner experimentation and incidental learning, allowing students to engage with concepts visually, kinetically, and orally. This multi-faceted approach not only enriches their understanding but also ignites their curiosity.

I firmly believe in Vygotsky's Zone of Proximal Development and the concept of scaffolding. In today's rapidly evolving world, particularly during the 4th Industrial Revolution, critical thinking skills are essential. My teaching methods are designed to challenge students while providing them with the necessary support to thrive.

As an educator, I pride myself on being resourceful and adaptable. I embrace difficult challenges with enthusiasm and perseverance, always striving to find innovative solutions that benefit my students.

In addition to my teaching career, I am an avid writer with several children's books to my name. My love for poetry and literature extends into my personal interests in anthropology, enriching my perspective as both an educator and a creative individual.

Sincerely,

Gabriella Da Costa